The Cr

(The Ronnie and Bernard Adventures Book One)

By Jason Ayres

With additional material by Michael Livesley

Text copyright © 2022 Jason Ayres
All Rights Reserved

This is a work of fiction. Names, characters, businesses, places, events and incidents are either the products of the author's imagination or used in a fictitious manner. Any resemblance to actual persons, living or dead, or actual events is purely coincidental.

Based on the characters of Ronnie Rathbone and Bernard Bradshaw, created by Jason Ayres, Paul Carmichael, and Michael Livesley.

Contents

Prologue 1
Chapter One 4
Chapter Two 27
Chapter Three 51
Chapter Four 75
Chapter Five 100
Chapter Six 126
Chapter Seven 142
Chapter Eight 165
Chapter Nine 185
Chapter Ten 204
Chapter Eleven 221
Chapter Twelve 236

Prologue
2000 BC (approx.)

On a warm summer night, thousands of years ago, a group of robed Druids were offering up a sacrifice to their gods.

Dressed all in black, the five subordinate members of the group were standing in front of five large stones. The huge rocks were of the same type as the bluestones used to build Stonehenge. Despite the stones weighing several tons each, the primitive people of the time had managed to transport them a great distance, from the Preseli Hills in South Wales to their current location in what would one day become central England.

The stones formed the crude shape of a pentagon and surrounded a larger flat slab, to which the Druids' intended victim was securely attached.

Each Druid was carrying a flaming torch, illuminating the hapless victim. In front of them was the group's high priest who was presiding over a dais at the head of the slab. Like the others, he was dressed in robes with his face completely covered, but there was one key difference. This man was dressed all in white, denoting his status as the leader. Above his head he held a bronze dagger, the sharp blade aimed squarely at the victim below.

Unlike the Druids, the man on the slab was sparsely dressed in just a tunic and a torn white shirt which exposed his chest. The open shirt revealed a gold necklace, which contained a striking red jewel. He was tightly bound by both legs and arms to all four corners of the rock, and lay calm, showing no signs of struggling against his bonds. It appeared that he had accepted his fate, as his face also betrayed no signs of fear. If anything it was the opposite, as he lay there with a defiant smirk.

His relaxed attitude was angering the Druids who were being denied the opportunity to gloat over the fear and pain of the man they were about to execute. To the casual observer, it might have appeared that they were evil and vindictive men, but that was not the case at all. They had never committed a human sacrifice before but the events leading up to this moment had left them with no alternative.

They were carrying out this execution as much for their own protection as anything else. The man on the slab before them had committed the vilest imaginable offences against their people, including the murder of women and children. He had been ruthless and they were in no doubt that if they did not do this now, he would destroy them all.

"Kill him, kill him, kill him!" chanted the Druids in unison, many of whom had lost their loved ones at the hands of the evil creature that lay before them.

The high priest raised his hand to signal that they should fall quiet, and then he began to speak.

"Vile demon Fendara, you have heard the list of crimes carried out against our tribespeople. The sentence is death! You shall be sacrificed this Midsummer's day to appease our gods and beg for their mercy as we cast your evil from within our midst. Do you have anything to say?"

The man he had called Fendara cackled with laughter, almost as if he were revelling in the moment. It was not the demeanour of a man who knew he was facing certain death.

"Primitive fools! Do you think you can destroy me that easily? I shall scatter my essence throughout time and when the moment arrives for my return, your descendants will wish they had never been born!"

The high priest had heard enough. He and the others had seen enough to suggest that Fendara possessed incredible demonic powers that they could not understand. They had witnessed him perform feats such as firing lightning bolts from his fingertips that could kill at a distance.

Despite their intended victim being tightly bound, the priest dared not delay the sacrifice any longer. With the powers that he had previously witnessed, he could not rule out the demon conjuring up some new magic to evade his execution. Without further pomp or ceremony, he plunged the dagger squarely into Fendara's chest.

The Druids cheered as the evil entity's body stiffened briefly, then went limp. The evil that had terrorised their land for so long was vanquished. Or was it? Staring at the body, they were shocked to see the red jewel in the necklace begin to glow, brighter than any star in the sky. Then it slowly faded away into nothingness. Shortly afterwards, the seemingly dead body also began to turn translucent and disappear.

Within a few seconds, it was as if Fendara had never been there.

Chapter One
June 1972

In the office of a small northern handbag factory, a discussion was taking place between the owner and his deputy.

The office was spartan, dull and grey. The manager, Mr Crispin, was lounging back in a faded black leather chair that had seen better days, smoking a large King Edward cigar. He was immaculately dressed, if a little old-fashioned for the 1970s, in a double-breasted navy suit, matching waistcoat, and red bowtie.

He was seated behind a grandiose wooden desk, which was at least twice as large as it needed to be given the paucity of things on it. In addition to the glass ashtray into which he was flicking his cigar, there was a black, leather-bound diary and an expensive-looking Parker pen. Both had the initials *CC* engraved upon them. The only other item was a standard-issue GPO 746 telephone, in an uninspiring shade of grey. There was no paperwork of any kind. Mr Crispin had other people do all of that for him. He just gave the orders, which was the way he liked it.

There was one other notable thing in the room and that was a depressing-looking sales chart on the wall behind him. It contained a single black line, with jagged ups and downs. There was no denying the fact that there were more downs than up and the overall trend was heading towards the bottom right-hand corner of the graph. Or at least it had been. Nobody had bothered to update the monthly figures since April 1971.

The office was square and took up one corner of the factory floor. It had been boxed off with thin chipboard panels and glass windows. Through one of these windows to the left of the desk, several machinists could be seen stitching zips onto the firm's signature product, the Royal Widnes handbag.

On the opposite side of the desk was Tommy, who supervised the factory floor. The difference between the men couldn't have been more stark. Tommy very much fitted the archetypal image of the working-class man, in his blue overalls and flat cap. He had a small pencil tucked behind his ear. His chair was wooden and basic and set considerably lower than Mr Crispin's. Tommy was the shorter of the two men to begin with, and this seating arrangement merely emphasised the difference in stature between them, both physically and socially.

Tommy began to address his boss, somewhat nervously. He was conscious that his superior never took bad news well. And lately, there had been a lot of bad news.

"Mr Crispin, last week's shipment to Ainley's Accessories has been sent back. They say the bags are no good. Apparently, the zips keep sticking or something."

The response, as Tommy had expected, was not good. It was delivered in the haughty and pompous manner that Mr Crispin was well known for.

"Again? That's the third time this month. I'm not having it, I tell you! We are the finest purveyors of ladies' handbags in the land! That Ainley is a rogue, he always has been."

"Thing is, he's right though, boss. I checked them myself. It's those cheap zips you've started importing from the Far East. We can't keep cutting quality like this."

"We got to reduce costs, Tommy. You told me only yesterday that the women on the shop floor are demanding an eight per cent pay rise."

"Yes, well, it's all down to rising inflation. They reckon they can get a better deal elsewhere. That shop steward, Vera, means business. She says they'll leave if you don't pay it."

"I don't have the money for it, I'm afraid. There just doesn't seem to be the demand for our traditional accoutrements anymore. I blame all this feminist business myself. And we're not the only ones. I had lunch with Mr McDougall from the ladies' underwear factory the other day and he's very worried about this bra-burning nonsense. His figures are right down."

"Our figures will be even worse if word gets out we're peddling shoddy goods. Some woman in the pub at lunchtime was complaining about there being a hole in the bottom of her bag, and guess what? It was one of ours. I'm telling you, boss, we're in trouble!"

Mr Crispin got up from his desk, walked around to where Tommy was seated and looked him squarely in the eye.

"You're right, of course, Tommy. I've been trying to play it down because I didn't want to worry you and the girls out there. But the truth is, if we can't turn this around soon, Crispin's is going to go bankrupt and this place will close – forever!"

At the conclusion of Mr Crispin's speech, both he and Tommy turned and stared dramatically directly into a large camera. This occupied the right-hand side of the office where an external wall ought to have been.

"And, cut!" shouted the director, from further behind the camera. "That's it for tonight, it's 10pm."

The rest of the crew in the TV studio relaxed and began to pack up as the two actors who had been playing Mr Crispin and Tommy walked off the set. The office they had just vacated had only two walls. The other two sides were used for filming purposes. It was just a small part of the much larger main factory set which was the principal setting for the thrice-weekly teatime soap opera, *Sladen Square*, in which they starred.

Ronnie Rathbone, the actor who portrayed Mr Crispin, strode purposefully across the studio, aware as ever that there was a narrow window of drinking time between the ending of filming and the closing of the studio bar.

He was a tall man who strode with an air of confidence, though some might have interpreted it as arrogance. He had a suspiciously lush head of hair for a man of his age, though to be fair, nobody was sure exactly how old he was. He claimed to be in his mid-forties, but many suspected he was on the wrong side of fifty.

Ronnie considered himself a cut above the other actors and frequently stated that he had only lowered himself to starring in a soap opera as a quick stopgap between gigs at The Old Vic. This temporary arrangement had lasted eight years so far.

His co-star, Bernard 'Barrel of Laughs' Bradshaw had been on the show a shorter time, and couldn't have been more different. He was an up-and-coming comedian from a working-class background who was well known on the northern circuit. He had sold out venues across the north of England in the past couple of years, as well as starring in his own sitcom. Ronnie, who claimed to be of noble heritage, considered both these things to be common and made sure that Bernard knew it.

Bernard was younger by several years, and Ronnie made frequent references to this, often addressing him as 'boy'. He saw the younger man as a threat and refused to be upstaged by someone who was from his perspective an oik who needed to be kept in his place. He refused to entertain the possibility that Bernard was the rising star and an audience favourite, whilst his star was very much on the wane.

Thus far his strategy, at least within the confines of the *Sladen Square* family, had been a successful one. That was despite what the press might have been saying, but he never read the papers. As far as he was concerned, when they came together on set Bernard was very much his junior. It helped that the younger man had recently split up with his wife, Diane, the love of his life. The breakup had left him riddled with angst and self-doubt, a situation that Ronnie mercilessly exploited at every possible opportunity.

Anyone watching could have seen straightaway what the established hierarchy was between the pair of them as they made their way off the set. As Ronnie strode boldly in the direction of the bar, Bernard was scurrying along nervously in his wake.

"Are you, er, going for a pint in the bar then, Ronnie?"

Bernard's question brought an instant look of annoyance to Ronnie's face. He had been looking forward to knocking back a few brandies in the bar after a long night's filming and the last thing he wanted was the prospect of listening to Bernard whingeing on about Diane again.

"No. I've um, got to see a man about a dog, Bernie my boy. Sorry about that."

He tapped his nose knowingly, to try to create the impression he had some important business that was above Bernard's station. With any luck, the peasant would give up and go home.

"Oh, right. I didn't realise. I mean, you usually go to the bar. Thing is, I wanted to see if you could give me a bit of advice about Diane, but I suppose if you're not going to be there, I could talk to Verity instead."

It was no good. His lie about not going to the bar was no use if Bernard was going there anyway and he certainly wasn't missing his after-show drinks just to keep up the pretence. He also didn't want Bernard talking to Verity who would doubtless badmouth him behind his back. He would have to go along and listen to the boy wittering on, but at least he could try to get a few drinks out of it.

"Oh for fu… fine. Come on then, but you're buying if I am going to have to endure yet another instalment of your lovesick saga."

The two of them made their way along the long corridor beyond the studio which led to the bar, with Ronnie power walking, such was his enthusiasm to obtain his first drink of the evening. When they arrived they saw that it was very crowded, as it often was on a Friday evening. Many of the actors and programme makers from the regional ITV station that employed them were relaxing after an evening's filming.

There was always a rush on at this time, as union rules dictated that all filming must be completed by 10pm on all shows. If it wasn't in the can by then, it wasn't happening. The unions were very strong in the land of television and everything ran to a very strict routine. Frequent strikes took place, the most recent in an argument over extra payments for colour television. Consequently, several episodes of *Sladen Square* the previous year had been produced and broadcast in black and white.

Once they had acquired their drinks, a large brandy for Ronnie and a lemonade for Bernard, they made their way to a small table where Bernard attempted to engage Ronnie in conversation over the sorry state of his love life. He did not, however, find a sympathetic ear. Far from offering any comfort, Ronnie preferred to make light of the situation, as well as boasting about his past exploits with various women. This was done to make Bernard feel even more inadequate.

"So I said to her, you call that a chopper? This is a chopper!"

Ronnie delivered this punchline just as Verity, the young, dark-haired costume designer who Bernard had mentioned earlier, approached the table. She overheard the end of the exchange and threw a snarky look at Ronnie. There was no love lost between the two of them.

Ronnie either didn't notice or chose to ignore the look, adapting as usual the condescending tone he used with all people he considered himself superior to. With his delusions of grandeur, this amounted to just about anyone who wasn't royalty.

"Oh hello, Verity. What do you want? Haven't you got any costumes to be sewing or anything?"

Verity looked daggers at him, but she avoided rising to the bait. She wasn't getting into a row with him now, there had been enough of that in the past. She would feign politeness because she had something she needed to discuss with them both. In addition, she had an important message for Bernard alone.

"Hello, Rathbone. Hello, Bernard. I'm glad I caught you. Are either of you striking next week?"

"Certainly not, the bloody workshy shower of..." began Ronnie before Verity interrupted him to explain further.

"Equity is campaigning to stop the station exploiting you actors by getting you off weekly contracts. They are demanding you be given long-term ones instead. In the case of the main cast of *Sladen Square*, that means at least an annual retainer, possibly more."

On hearing this, and realising it was to his benefit, Ronnie immediately changed his tone and completed his previous sentence.

"As I was saying ...fine, proud upstanding comrades. Count me in."

Verity rolled her eyes at Ronnie's blatant about-turn. The man was transparent and shallow beyond belief and she couldn't understand why Bernard seemed to idolise him so much. He had been through a tough time and she couldn't imagine that Ronnie was being of much comfort. To make matters worse, she had come to deliver at least one piece of news, possibly two, that was going to inflict more pain upon him.

"By the way, Bernard, I passed on your message to Diane. I'm sorry, love, but she doesn't want to talk to you."

"I heard she had gone back to that boring-looking bastard that she was with before you," said Ronnie.

Verity had maintained an air of civility up to this point, but she couldn't allow that comment to pass unchallenged. Talk about kicking a man when he was down.

"You're the bastard, Ronnie! Bernard needs our support, not the likes of you putting him down all the time."

"Your claims of illegitimacy are false, my dear. There is none of that in my heritage. My grandfather was a baronet, I'll have you know. Besides, it's high time the boy faced reality. She's gone, and she's not coming back."

While Ronnie was making this little declaration he was waving his brandy glass around theatrically in front of him, but he overdid it and it slipped out of his hand and smashed on the floor.

"Oops! Good job it was nearly empty."

Bernard leapt up, eager to rectify the situation.

"I'll get them in," he declared before heading up to the bar, leaving Verity alone with Ronnie.

"You really are an insufferable arsehole, Rathbone," she said.

"Yes. I know. But what can you, a mere costume designer, do about it?"

Verity was furious but knew there was an element of truth in what he had said. Ronnie was by no means the only actor she had come across in her career who treated those they looked down on with disdain, especially women. She longed for a day when that would change and men like him would no longer be able to get away with their vile behaviour, but now was not the time for that fight. Right now, she still had pressing business with Bernard which she feared was going to further add to his woes.

Without saying another word, she gave Ronnie a filthy look and got up from the table. She followed Bernard to the bar where he was ordering the next round of drinks. Away from Ronnie, she might be able to have a proper conversation with him.

"Bernard, I'm sorry, love, but this telegram was delivered to your dressing room when you were on set. I hate to add to your troubles but it's got a black edge to it."

"What does that mean?"

"Well, it usually means that somebody has died."

"Oh, great. That's all I need on top of everything else."

Back at the table, Ronnie was waiting impatiently for his brandy and smoking a Peter Stuyvesant cigarette when he looked up to see an unwelcome figure approaching.

The Colonel was the local bookmaker, amongst other things. Ronnie didn't know his real name. Rumours of links to the criminal underworld were probably not unfounded and he looked every inch the part. He was impeccably dressed in an incredibly expensive-looking Italian suit, topped off with a trilby.

He was accompanied by two extremely burly-looking gentlemen who would not have looked out of place at the door of one of Manchester's seedier nightclubs.

The Colonel was a man to be feared and had Ronnie quaking in his boots right now, but he had no intention of showing it. He knew why he was here and for the moment he was just going to have to brazen out the situation. For once he wished Bernard was by his side for moral support, not that the little pipsqueak would be much use against the two heavies if things turned nasty.

"Good evening, Ronald, what an absolute delight to see you."

He was one of the politest people that Ronnie had ever met, and that was one of the things that made him so scary. Every word he uttered had a hint of menace in it, even if he was saying something nice. He was the sort of man who would send your mother flowers on her birthday, before having you beaten to a pulp down a back alley.

"Good evening, Colonel. How did you get in here? This bar is for members only."

"Oh, I know the fellow on the door, used to be a runner for me in the sixties. Speaking of runners, where did you get to the other night? You said you were going to the Gents and then you'd settle your account. Then, lo and behold, you didn't come back. A gentleman always pays his gambling debts. Am I to take it that you're not a gentleman?"

"Good heavens no, what happened was…"

"Now you wouldn't be about to try and pull the wool over my eyes, would you? I find deception upsets my stomach, and that upsets Charlie here, isn't that right, Charles?"

The heavy by the name of Charlie glared at Ronnie with violent intent and gave a Neanderthal grunt of acknowledgement which wouldn't have been out of place in *Planet of the Apes*.

"Yes, I can see that," said Ronnie, trying to bluster things out. "That must be very distressing for you. Maybe you should take a couple of Rennies or something."

"It's readies we need to talk, my friend, not Rennies. Five thousand of them, to be precise. So, what are we going to do about it?"

Ronnie was granted a temporary respite as Verity returned to the table. He knew that the Colonel had a policy of never discussing business when there were ladies present.

"Ahh, Rupert. We haven't seen you down here in simply ages, come and meet the rest of the cast. I see you know Rathbone."

So that was his name, thought Ronnie. No wonder he didn't let it be put about. It didn't exactly suit the image.

"Sadly, yes," replied the Colonel, in response to her question about Ronnie. "But listen, we're right in the middle of a spot of business here."

"But I insist!" she exclaimed, grabbing him by the arm and attempting to manoeuvre him over to a much larger table where a group of Ronnie's co-stars were laughing and joking. As she dragged the Colonel away, he looked back to Ronnie to let him know their business wasn't concluded.

"Well, if you insist. Don't go anywhere, Ronald. I'll be back shortly."

The two heavies followed their boss away from the table, just as Bernard returned with the drinks.

"Who was that?" he asked.

"Oh, er, an agent. From the National, yes. He was trying to sign me up to do *Hamlet* again."

Bernard could tell that Ronnie was lying. He wasn't naïve enough not to have realised by now that half of what came out of Ronnie's mouth was pure fabrication.

"He didn't look like an agent. And I'm sure I've seen those two well-built fellows that were with him before. They look like the blokes I saw giving some lad a right going over outside the back of the Mecca last Saturday. You've not been gambling again, have you?"

"Of course not, dear fellow. What do you take me for, some sort of addict? You're the one with the booze problem."

"This isn't about me, and I'm talking about gambling, not drinking. I thought you would have learned your lesson after that incident with the church silver last year."

"Alleged incident, my boy, alleged incident. Nothing was ever proved."

"If I recall rightly, the producer insisted you attend Gamblers Anonymous afterwards."

"Waste of time! Full of lily-livered losers bleating out their bleeding-heart life stories. I get enough of that from you."

"So you did go?"

"Only once, and the damned thing overran by an hour which meant I was late getting to the betting shop. When I got there I discovered I'd missed a 16/1 winner at Chepstow. After that, I swore never again."

"You've definitely got a problem, mate."

"Rubbish! Gambling addicts are weak-willed mortals who can't help themselves. We Rathbones are made of sterner stuff. We have this little thing called willpower. Let me assure you, Ronald 'Kitchener' Rathbone is immune to addictions."

As he finished his sentence, he took a long draw on his by now almost spent cigarette, stubbed it out in the ashtray, and looked impatiently at Bernard who was still clutching the drinks.

"You did get me a large one, didn't you?"

"Of course. When do you ever have anything else?"

"Well hand it over then. We've digressed, so just to re-emphasise, that fellow was just an agent and you might like to know that I said no. My place is here, Bernard. By your side in your hour of need."

After making his blatantly insincere utterance, Ronnie took a large swig of his brandy before muttering quietly under his breath so Bernard couldn't hear, "as long as you keep the drinks coming."

"Thank you, Ronnie, I appreciate it."

"What's that you're clutching, by the way?" said Ronnie, noticing for the first time the telegram that Bernard had tucked under his arm while he was carrying the drinks.

"Telegram, arrived earlier," replied Bernard. He opened it and began to read the contents.

"Telegram, eh? Takes me back to my days in Malaya. I recall receiving word from Peter Hall that he wanted me to take over from Larry in *Coriolanus*. Of course, I refused. Country comes first, what?"

"Bloody hell," said Bernard, who hadn't been listening to Ronnie's waffle as he had been concentrating on the contents of the message.

"What's the matter? It's not from Peter Hall, is it? Now that would be a turn-up."

"No, it's from a solicitor. It says that my Uncle Arthur has died."

"Oh, my deepest condolences, dear boy. Were you close?"

"Hardly. I didn't even know I had an Uncle Arthur. According to this, he was a lord."

"I highly doubt that going by your common upbringing. Perhaps it's a misprint. Maybe they meant to say lard."

"Oh, my! You're not going to believe this!" said Bernard in an excited tone.

"What? He hasn't died and left you his gas bill, has he?"

"No, quite the reverse. He's left me his entire estate."

On hearing this, Ronnie's attitude switched from flippant to interested. If Bernard had come into some money then, well, he was Bernard's best friend, wasn't he? It stood to reason that he would want to share his good fortune.

"Well, this calls for a celebration. How about some champagne, assuming Tommy Cooper hasn't drunk the place dry of it? Oh, sorry, you're off the sauce, aren't you?"

"You know I am."

"The edicts of the ex-wife again, eh? Well, in my opinion, you're well rid. Any woman who demanded I gave up my perfectly reasonable refreshment requirements would be given short shrift, I can tell you."

"Yes, well I'm not like you, am I? I was committed to making a proper go of my marriage. Unlike you."

"Ah well, chin up, old boy, how much has he left you? A few quid and his gold teeth? You want to get them out before the undertakers get their hands on them."

"It says I need to go down there to find out."

"And where might that be?"

"A village called Weirdwell in Shroudshire. I've been invited to attend the reading of the will."

"And when is this prestigious gathering, do tell?"

"This Sunday. Well, that's that, I can't go."

"What? Why? What could you possibly have to do on a Sunday that could be more important? This could change your whole life. In fact, I shall dust the mothballs off the old Jensen and drive you there myself."

"No, you don't understand. This Sunday is Diane's birthday. I was going to go round there with flowers and chocolates to show her how much I appreciate her."

"For God's sake, Bernard, listen. Diane is history. She's shacked up with that sound engineer she was sleeping with before she met you. Rumour has it she never really stopped. Now, my advice is that you move on, go to the will reading, and I shall be by your side all the way."

"No, Ronnie. Diane is my priority. If I could just get her to see that I've changed, things can go back to how they were before."

"She's divorced you! What more evidence do you need that it's over? Finished! Kaput! Now, just stop for a minute and think about it. If this uncle of yours really was a lord he could have left you an absolute fortune. You need to forget about Diane, get down to your dead uncle's pile and then you can ascend to the sunlit uplands."

"You think money can make me happy? Let me make it clear. There will be no sunlit uplands without Diane, no matter how much he's left me."

"Use your loaf, lad. She doesn't want you in your current sorry state. But she might feel differently once you're rich. You might even have inherited a title. What woman could resist a lord? I'm of noble blood, myself, you know. Have I ever mentioned that?"

"On numerous occasions. And anyway, Diane's not like that. She's no gold digger. I'm a rising star. If she was after money, why would she have left me for someone on the crew? I've got far more earning potential than him."

"Not if you carry on like this you haven't. Call yourself a comedian? You won't be making many people laugh if you keep going around all day with a face as long as the Mersey Tunnel. Now, I suggest you give this some serious thought while I go and strain the greens, I shan't be long."

Frustrated with Bernard's refusal to listen to reason, Ronnie walked off to the toilets. There must be some way of getting through to Bernard that his ex-wife didn't want him anymore. As he urinated in quiet contemplation, he came up with a plan.

Instead of going straight back to the table, he went to the bar and concealed himself behind a pillar, out of sight of Bernard. Attracting the barmaid's attention, he asked for the telephone and then pulled out a notebook. It had a picture of himself on it, crudely plastered next to another of Laurence Olivier, to make it look as if they were on stage together. He flicked through it, located the number he was looking for and made the call.

"Hello, Diane? Yes, it's Ronnie. How are you?"

He paused for a moment, listening to her response before continuing. She didn't sound overjoyed to hear from him, but he hadn't expected her to be, under the circumstances.

"Listen, you know I'm not one to stick my nose in, but I have heard that Bernard is planning on coming around this Sunday and surprising you with flowers for your birthday."

It was a bad line, but what she said in reply was music to his ears. She didn't want Bernard anywhere near her, which suited Ronnie's plans down to the letter.

"Yes, well I thought it was a bad idea too. Diane, I have told him, but he won't listen. My advice to you is to make sure he is left in no doubt whatsoever that it is over. If you are happy for me to shock him into reality then I will tell him."

She asserted her agreement which was all he needed to hear.

"Thank you. I'll break the bad news to him now."

He hung up, feeling rather pleased with himself. She didn't want him, which meant Bernard would be more vulnerable than ever. All he had to do was play his cards right, and old Arthur's riches would be as good as his. Then he wouldn't have to worry about the Colonel and his two pet Rottweilers anymore.

Returning to his seat, he finalised his plan. He had decided against passing on the message from Diane. If he did that, Bernard would want to know why he had rung her in the first place and he didn't have a good answer for that. No, he needed something far more devastating. Something that would get the message across once and for all. And he had come up with the perfect idea. It was a little cruel, even by his standards, but what was it they said? You had to be cruel to be kind? It was time to test that theory out.

"Well, that was interesting," he said.

"What was?" replied Bernard, who was sitting glumly in his seat nursing his lemonade.

"You know you've got so boring since you stopped drinking. Why don't you have just one? You might need it, bearing in mind what I'm about to tell you."

"No, Ronnie. The next drink I have will be a glass of champagne on the day Diane and I remarry, and not before."

"Suit yourself. I just thought it might soften the blow."

"What blow?"

"I've just seen that sound engineer in the bog, you know the one that's been knocking off your ex."

"That bastard! You know, he never stopped sniffing around her, even after we got married."

"Well, you ought to brace yourself, old boy. He was handing around the cigars in there and telling all the chaps the good news."

"What good news?"

"I'm sorry to break it to you, but when I said knocking off, perhaps I should have said knocking up. Diane's pregnant."

"What!" exclaimed Bernard, sitting up straight in his chair, with a look of shock on his face. Then the red mist began to descend.

"Afraid so, old sausage, expecting a little engineer in the spring."

"I'm not standing for this! Is he still in there? I'll rip his bloody spine out!"

Bernard leapt up, determined to seek revenge, but Ronnie grabbed his arm to restrain him. Since he had made the entire thing up, there was no point in Bernard rushing off to confront someone who wasn't there.

"You're too late, I'm afraid. He was about to jump in a cab with a couple of cameramen. He said they were going clubbing in Salford to celebrate. Now look, I know you must be devastated, but I think you should see this as a sign that it's time to move on to pastures new."

"How can I? I think this latest revelation is going to be the final straw that absolutely destroys me."

"I know, old stick, but look on the bright side. She's his problem now. You've had a lucky escape if you ask me."

Bernard slumped back into his chair, staring into space in stunned silence, as he contemplated the situation. What was he going to do?

Ronnie had only one goal in mind and that was to get Bernard to the will reading on Sunday. He was going to have to get him to snap out of it. Leaning across the table, he took him by surprise by slapping him cleanly across the face.

"What did you do that for?" said Bernard, stunned.

"Because I love you, old darling, and I can't bear to see you suffering so. That was an act of kindness to shock you out of your misery. You must forget Diane and move on. And that process of moving on will begin on Sunday at the reading of the will. I know you say she's not a gold digger, but face it, you'll be a much more attractive proposition once you've inherited a title. Who knows, maybe you can all live happily ever after in your late uncle's stately pile."

"Do you really think so?"

"Of course. Assuming you don't mind someone else's sprog's dirty nappies stinking out the place."

"I can't believe she's having someone else's baby. You know, I honestly feel right now like my life is over."

"On the contrary, old man, it's only just beginning. Trust me, the reading of this will on Sunday could be the beginning of a whole new adventure."

"I guess so. Thanks for coming along tonight, Ronnie, I know you had other plans. I don't care what anyone says, you're a true pal."

"Don't mention it. What are friends for? Right, I must be going. I shall pick you up on Sunday morning."

He had been encouraged by Bernard's last remark. It seemed like he had been getting through to him, but as soon as he got up, he could that he was once again staring vacantly into space. He was going to have his work cut out to keep him on track.

"Hey, dopey!" he said, clicking his fingers right in front of Bernard's face. "See you on Sunday!"

"Right, yes, Sunday."

Hopeful that the weekend's plans were now set in stone, Ronnie wandered over to the bar, where the Colonel was ordering more drinks for him and his two assistants. Dealing with Bernard had been relatively straightforward, but now came the difficult bit. He hoped he could prevail on the Colonel to be patient while he got his hands on some of Bernard's loot.

"Colonel, I shall have your money a week from today," he announced confidently.

"Next Friday?"

"Correct. Would you prefer cash or cheque?"

"Cash, of course. Though another week will add a further two hundred and fifty to the balance, I'm afraid. It's the inflation, you know."

"Ah, yes, that darned inflation. Funnily enough, we had a scene in the show tonight talking about just that. But it's not a problem. I'm good for it."

"Very good. But just so we all know where we stand I must caution you that if you don't pay up next Friday then Charles and Kenneth here will be more than happy to help you assist with the building of the M62, if you understand what I mean?"

"Whatever you say, Colonel."

"Good," he replied, turning back to the bar to indicate that the conversation was over.

Ronnie was quite pleased with the way the evening had gone and decided it was time he was on his way. Acting was in his blood, and just as he always liked to make a dramatic entrance, he also felt that a strong exit was important for a man of his standing. As he made the way to the door, passing the table of his cast mates, he made sure he announced his departure loudly.

"Goodbye, everybody, goodbye. It's been an absolute pleasure to have your company again on this fine summer's eve, but all good things must come to an end. Let us part, dear friends, and do it all again soon."

The response from the table was lukewarm at best. Some of them barely acknowledged him, including some jobbing older actress who played a cleaning lady who didn't even stop talking as he was giving his farewell speech. Bloody heathens. He was the star of the show. How dare they disrespect him like this? He might have to suggest to the producer that they cull some of these minor characters and focus more on him.

Just before he got to the door, he encountered Verity again, who was coming back from the Ladies.

"Goodbye, Verity," he said, not expecting much of a response, and he was right.

"Rathbone," she said disparagingly, before making a beeline once again for the Colonel. Was that all he was worth now? A disparaging utterance of his surname without so much as a goodnight? Still, who cared? Screw her! She was a nobody, and he was a huge star. Better still, if all his plans came to fruition, he would soon be a rich star. Of course, if he hadn't blown all his money on booze, gambling and womanising, he would already be one, but he preferred not to think about that.

As he left the building, emerging into the warm night air of a pleasant June evening, he had every reason to feel optimistic. He pulled his trusty hip flask out of his pocket, took a swig, and then jumped into the waiting taxi which he had insisted ferry him to and from the studio as part of his contract.

Sunday was going to be a good day.

Chapter Two
June 1972

The following morning, Ronnie was rudely awakened by the telephone ringing. He didn't take kindly to being disturbed early at the weekend, particularly after the copious amounts of brandy he had sunk the previous evening. After arriving home he had carried on drinking in front of some old Hammer Horror movie which had been the only thing he could find to watch on TV. It was some nonsense about a haunted house and ghosts terrorising unsuspecting visitors.

He considered such things to be utter hogwash. In his opinion, there was no such thing as ghosts. It was all idle superstition but he watched it anyway. It wasn't like he had anything better to do. It had been a couple of years now since his acrimonious split from the most recent Mrs Rathbone and he had lived alone in his flat ever since.

Having dragged himself out of bed to answer the phone, he was perturbed to discover it was the studio demanding that he come in for an urgent meeting with the producer. This was an unprecedented development on a Saturday. What did the old fart want? He agreed grudgingly, but only on the proviso they sent a cab for him.

He decided to dress in his country gentleman's outfit, as befitted a man of his status, so tweed was the order of the day. In some of his more far-fetched flights of fancy he imagined himself spending the weekends as a guest on a large country estate. He would spend the daytime shooting grouse with the gentry, and then in the evening would seduce the ladies with his dazzling conversation over dinner.

No such invitations were ever forthcoming, and his attire often attracted strange looks when strolling into the local branch of Peter Dominic which was where he bought his weekend bottle of brandy. It didn't bother him. What did he care what the commoners in there buying their cans of Skol thought of him?

What did annoy him was the constant pestering from *Sladen Square* viewers asking him for autographs. Every Saturday when he went to the local precinct to buy his provisions they were there, buying their cheap cuts of meat in the butchers and their loaves of sliced white bread in the corner shop.

He found the whole food shopping business to be a frightful experience. He did not consider it to be a manly thing to do, but he had no choice due to his current status of being between wives. He bought the absolute bare minimum to see him through the week and barely cooked at all, getting most of his meals in the staff restaurant at work. He only used small local shops and had never set foot in one of the big, modern supermarkets, which seemed daunting places. He wouldn't have known where to start with them.

Of late, the autograph requests had become less frequent but they were no less annoying. One middle-aged woman had particularly irked him the previous weekend by asking if he could get Bernard's autograph for her. She hadn't wanted his. He considered that to be the height of rudeness and was at the point where he was seriously tempted to tell some of them to fuck off.

He resisted the urge because it would probably get back to the press and he didn't want to attract their attention again. Whoever had coined the phrase 'there's no such thing as bad publicity' hadn't known what they were talking about, at least as far as he was concerned.

Today, because of the summons to the studio, the shopping would have to wait. By the time he was fully dressed and had performed his ablutions, he heard a couple of sharp beeps. He looked through the grimy window of his one-bedroomed ground-floor flat to see that the taxi was already outside.

By the front door, he found a hand-delivered letter on the mat. It was an eviction notice from his landlord, threatening that if he didn't pay up what he owed by teatime he would be thrown out of the flat. He decided to ignore it. It was doubtless just an empty threat and he would be rich soon anyway so what did he care? He could get a much bigger and nicer place than this dump.

It was mid-morning by the time he got to the producer's office, by which time he was feeling more like his old self. A hair of the dog from his hip flask in the back of the cab had sweetened his mood, and he was full of his usual bluster when he was ushered inside.

Terrance Oldman was a veteran of the commercial television world, having been at the station since ITV was launched in the mid-1950s. Greying, and wearing half-moon glasses, he looked to be north of seventy but was still going strong. When Ronnie entered he was playing around with a desk toy. It was one of those Newton's cradle things with five silver balls that swung back and forth like a pendulum making a constant, annoying clanking sound.

As Ronnie entered, Terrance looked up from the desk to greet him.

"Morning, Rathbone," he said cheerfully.

Ronnie removed his deerstalker hat and walked to the side of the room to place it on the hat stand. Whatever the old man wanted, he seemed to be in a good mood.

"You wanted to see me, Terrance? I trust it won't take too long. I'm playing croquet with the Duke of Kidderminster after lunch."

"Yes. I'm sorry to drag you in on a Saturday, but with the union calling everyone out on Monday, this won't wait."

"Not a problem, always a pleasure to see you, old fruit."

"And you, Ron. Now look, there's no easy way to say this so I'll just cut to the chase. The studio isn't planning on giving you a new contract when all this strike nonsense is resolved."

Ronnie couldn't believe what he was hearing and summoned up his most outraged tone for his response.

"What? But I've given *Sladen Square* the best years of my life!"

"Yes, and we are very grateful. But I'm sorry, my hands are tied. The truth is that we've done some audience research and we've decided we want the show to focus mainly on the character of Tommy going forward."

"You're joking!? You want to make that illiterate orangutan who can barely string three words together the main star? That, that, bloody comedian?"

"The public love him, though. Everyone loves a comedian."

"I don't think he's funny. I mean, the man has built his entire comedy career on the character of a stereotypical northerner who says, 'Ey up' a lot."

"Bernie 'Barrel of Laughs' Bradshaw is a hot property in the industry. Despite your low opinion of him, he's got a sell-out national tour coming up, not to mention the summer season at Blackpool Tower."

"Summer season? Blackpool? It's hardly the RSC, is it? I've performed in front of royalty. The Duke of York and Prince of Wales have both enjoyed my work."

"You know very well that those are the names of pubs and if I recall rightly you were banned from both. Now look, my hands are tied."

"Untie them, then."

"I can't. Look, I'll level with you. I've had my orders from upstairs."

"What, you mean Sir Sidney? I don't believe you. Only last week I was guest of honour at his birthday party."

"Yes, you were, I was there, remember?"

"Were you? I don't recall."

"You were probably too drunk. And presumably, you don't recall what you said."

"Oh, a few entertaining anecdotes, no doubt. Sir Sydney loves all that stuff."

"You started spouting some outdated rubbish about a woman's place being in the home."

"Oh, yes, that, all said in jest. Anyway, Sir Sydney loved it. He was laughing."

"Maybe he was, but his wife wasn't. She had a face like thunder and gave him hell afterwards. And to compound it all, you then handed her an empty plate and asked her to wash it up. To say that didn't go down well would be the understatement of the year."

"Oh, it'll be fine. I'll send her some flowers or something, that will sort it."

"I very much doubt it. But that aside, you still can't deny the findings of our market research. Here at QTV, we need to move with the times. Mass market appeal is what it's all about, and we need to give the audience what they want."

"Yes, and I'm telling you, when they settle down in the evenings to watch a bit of telly, they don't want to be confronted with some third-rate comedian. They want to see class and quality. They want to watch a classically trained actor. Barrel of laughs? Scraping the bottom of the biscuit barrel, more like. Dreadful."

"Look, it's not that you aren't talented…"

"Multi-talented, I'll have you know. Not a one-trick pony like him."

Terrance ignored the interruption and continued his sentence from where he left off.

"…but this isn't just about that or popularity. You've upset several of the staff on the show."

"Oh, that bloody Verity been bleating again, has she? Ignore her, the poor girl has got an unrequited crush on me."

"No, she hasn't. You've been condescending and sexist towards her on countless occasions. And that's not just her word against yours, a lot of people have picked up on it. Also, you've breached your contract on numerous occasions. Speaking of which you've also not been going to your Gamblers Anonymous meetings, and that was a term of your employment after your 'incident'."

"Let me correct you there. I have been going. I have lined up faithfully with that bunch of derelicts outside the Methodist church every Thursday for the last six months. And I have the photographs to prove it."

"Yes, but you didn't go inside, did you?"

"No, well it isn't my fault that the start time clashes with opening time, is it? But technically, I went, according to your criteria."

As the conversation dragged on, Terrance's tone was becoming increasingly exasperated. He was becoming tired of Ronnie's infantile responses and was keen to bring the meeting to as amicable a conclusion as possible. That wasn't easy where Rathbone was concerned, as he knew from experience. Perhaps he could offer some sort of loose compromise to soften the blow.

"I'm sorry, we've given you more than your fair share of second chances and you've blown them, but listen. We've decided we aren't going to kill Mr Crispin off. I was thinking perhaps we could get you in for the occasional guest appearance, perhaps if the other stars are off sick or unavailable for some reason. The audience will appreciate you more when you pop up. Absence makes the heart grow fonder, and all that."

"Off sick? It's only because my gout kept me off for three weeks that this buffoon got so big a part in the first place. You said he'd just be keeping my seat warm."

"It is what it is. Look, we've tried to do our best for you. We don't want to see you fall on hard times."

"Oh, don't you worry about me, I'll be alright. I had a call from my agent this morning offering me the *Morecambe and Wise Christmas Show*."

"That's great. I'm pleased for you. It sounds like you probably won't need that recurring role with us after all, then."

"You can shove your recurring role. You'll be crawling on your hands and knees for me to come back once I'm a huge star and then I shall take great delight in telling you where to go! Good day!"

With that he stormed out, leaving Terrance speechless. It had been an uncomfortable conversation for the ageing producer, but not an unprecedented one. Ronnie was difficult at the best of times. Still, he had achieved his objective to get him off the show and now hopefully that would be the end of it.

Ten seconds later, Ronnie flung the door open again and strode back in, much to Terrance's alarm. Was it not the end of it? Had he come back for more?

"I forgot my hat!" declared Ronnie, grabbing his deerstalker, and making his second dramatic exit in less than a minute.

If Ronnie thought he was having a bad day, it was nothing compared to Bernard's. He had gone home in absolute pieces the previous evening, after Ronnie's revelations in the bar. The thought of Diane carrying someone else's child had cut into the very heart of his being like a lethal dagger and he had cried himself to sleep well into the small hours.

Of course, he had no idea that Ronnie had made up the whole pregnancy story, but ultimately it made no difference to the status of the relationship. With child or not, she still didn't want him.

He had been sorely tempted when he got home to just say sod it and sink a bottle of whisky. It had been several months since he had touched alcohol, his excessive drinking being one of the reasons Diane had left him in the first place. There was still plenty of booze in the house. He liked having the temptation at hand as it strengthened his resolve to resist it. This went against all the advice he had been given, but it worked for him.

He wasn't sure if he would ever drink again. Was he an alcoholic? He didn't know, yet. He wasn't even sure what the precise definition of an alcoholic was. Would he ever be able to enjoy a drink in moderation again, or was that it now for good? The fact he was even having to ask these questions didn't bode well. He had never seen himself as the type to succumb to addictions. Was he an addict, or had the drinking been his way of coping with his failing marriage? And that then posed the chicken and egg question – which came first? The marriage problems or the drinking?

He lay in bed for some time mulling it over. Eventually, when he managed to find the will to drag himself out of bed, he trudged downstairs to the living room of his three-bed semi and went straight for the television. The curtains were still drawn, so he fumbled around in semi-darkness for the on/off button, switched it on and waited for the set to warm up. Then he plonked himself down on the sofa, to an unexpected crunching sound. He had sat down on some old takeaway boxes.

There was no denying it, the place was a tip. If a set designer had been asked to create the home of a man who had let himself go, he couldn't have made a better job of it. It was ridiculous to be living like this. He had earnt more money in the past couple of years than in the whole of his previous working life. He could easily afford to hire someone to clean the place up.

Perhaps that was the point. He didn't want to. Wallowing in squalor provided him with a certain degree of comfort. It didn't make any sense, but then nothing in his life did these days.

The TV was a waste of time. It was showing some boring cricket match between England and some other country, Australia, probably. He could only tell it was England because he recognised Geoff Boycott who was the only cricketer he knew. He considered it to be a boring game, not of interest to someone of his background. There had been no cricket at his school, just football in the playground, which he wasn't very good at. The war had been on during his schooldays, and sport hadn't been a priority.

He didn't bother changing the channel, what was the point? He wouldn't be able to concentrate on anything, all he could think about was Diane. Why had she done this to him? Why?

Full of remorse, he went back upstairs to the bedroom and opened the wardrobe to look for some clean clothes. No matter how miserable his mood was, he couldn't mope around in his Y-fronts all day. But he had nothing clean to wear. He would have to get something off the floor.

Maybe he ought to go to the launderette, or try to figure out how to use the washing machine. It had seemed so simple when Diane had done it. But when he looked at it, all he saw were dials with weird symbols and numbers on them. They might as well have been Egyptian hieroglyphics for all the sense they made to him.

What a mess his life was. What would his fans think of him if they could see him like this? He was the classic example of a tortured entertainer. All they saw was 'Barrel of Laughs' Bradshaw, the funny man who made them chuckle. There he was on the stage or the screen, laughing and joking on the outside, whilst all the while, slowly and silently dying on the inside. He thought about Tony Hancock and what had happened to him. Was he destined to meet the same fate?

There might not have been any clothes of his own in the wardrobe, but there were still some of Diane's. She had taken most of her stuff when she had left but had shown no interest in coming back for the rest, despite him sending messages to try to persuade her. He had been clinging to the idea that if only he could get her round to the house, he might be able to convince her to stay.

Well, there was no sign of that happening so what was he to do with her clothes? He wasn't about to start cross-dressing and was sick of the sight of seeing them every time he opened the door. They were a constant reminder of her. It was time to get rid of it all for good.

In the least dirty clothes of his own that he could find, he made his way out to the backyard. There was a large oil drum out there which he had used in the past to burn rubbish. He used some old papers and kindling and started a fire. Once it was established, he topped it up with some leftover coal from the previous winter. This was stored in a small bunker next to the door of the outside lavatory.

He ought to move out of this house. It had been built around the turn of the century and needed a lot of work done on it. It was old, and cold in the winter. He had bought it before he had found fame and he could easily afford to get it done up now. But he had no desire to do so. It held too many memories and he would be better off selling it and moving elsewhere.

He was going to begin the process of disposing of those memories right now. With the fire now blazing merrily away, he went back into the flat to make a start on what needed to be done.

He burnt the clothes first. She obviously didn't want them because she would have come back for them by now if she had. It was mostly older stuff anyway, late 1960s clothes that had gone out of fashion that she wouldn't want to wear anymore. Trends seemed to change so quickly in the modern world. As he put the items in, one by one, he wondered if he was being selfish doing this. He could have donated the clothes to charity. Never mind, it was too late now.

Then he heard some tutting from the other side of the brick wall separating his yard from the one next door. That would be old Mrs Johnson, who hadn't spoken to him since Diane left. It was clear whose side she was on. The tutting was followed by the sound of pegs being thrown loudly into a tin. Perhaps he should have checked she didn't have any washing out before he had started the fire, but to be fair, should he have been expected to? Everyone knew that Monday was washing day. Who put washing out on a Saturday?

Disposing of the clothes was the easy part. Now it was time for the painful bit. He opened an old tartan shortbread tin which was where he kept all his keepsakes of Diane.

One by one, he dropped memory after memory into the fire, tears rolling down his cheeks as he did. Black and white photographs of the pair of them in happier times, love letters she had written him in her beautiful italic handwriting, and even a faded newspaper article, with the headline 'TV's Golden Couple Tie the Knot'. All of it had to go.

Finally, he burnt the large bunch of flowers he had bought the previous day, intending to surprise Diane on her birthday. There was no way he could do that now. One by one, he picked off the petals and watched them flutter down into the flames within the drum.

When he went back into the house, he turned the radio on to try to take his mind off things. 'Without You' by Nilsson, which had recently spent several weeks at number one, was playing. It was the last thing he needed to hear. He turned the radio off, put on a bobble hat, wrapped a scarf around his face and went out for a walk. It was a ridiculous way to dress on a warm day in June but he couldn't cope with being recognised today. He would go for a long trek in the woods to try to take his mind off things.

The walk helped a lot. It was true what his gran used to say to him, fresh air and sunshine were the best medicine. Few people went to the woods he frequented when he wanted to clear his mind, just a few dog walkers, and there weren't many around today. He walked for miles, mulling things over in his mind. He knew realistically that it was over between him and Diane but his feelings for her ran so deep it was difficult to think objectively.

Perhaps the trip to Shroudshire tomorrow would help. He had to admit, he was intrigued by the mysterious telegram that had come out of the blue. There was quite a lot he didn't know about his family history. His mother had always been vague about it when he had asked and she was now long gone. He didn't have anyone else, having been an only child. No wonder he had become so dependent on Diane.

When he got back, he tidied up the flat a bit, then went out to get a takeaway curry before settling down to watch TV. There was very little on worth watching, and he had nothing better to do, so he ended up going to bed before it even got dark. So much for the glamorous lifestyles of the rich and famous.

The following morning, he was awoken by the repeated beeping of a car horn outside the front of the flat. He staggered out of bed and over the window to investigate the source of the commotion, only to see Ronnie impatiently blasting on the horn of his silver Jensen Interceptor. Great. That was all he needed and was hardly likely to improve Mrs Johnson's disposition towards him.

He managed to attract Ronnie's attention and gestured at him through the window to stop, before hastily throwing on the first items of clothes he could find scattered around on the floor. By the time he made it to the front door, Ronnie was waiting eagerly on the doorstep. A glance at the clock in the hallway showed it was only half past nine. Why had he come so early? The will reading wasn't until three o'clock.

"Ah, good morrow, sweet hero," said Ronnie, as Bernard opened the door. "Are we all ready to meet our destiny?"

Ronnie seemed remarkably cheerful for the early hour, and it didn't take Bernard long to work out why, as he detected a strong whiff of spirits in the air.

"Have you been drinking?" he inquired.

"I may have had a few sweet sherries over breakfast. I felt obliged to lubricate the wheels of celebration on your behalf, seeing as you have sworn off the stuff."

"That settles it then, I'm staying here. I'm beginning to regret burning those flowers now. Maybe I can get some more and take them round to Diane."

"Nonsense, I won't hear of it. You must accept the situation, Bernard. She has walked out of your life and into the arms of another. But better to have loved and lost than never to have loved at all, eh? Besides, where are you going to get flowers on a Sunday? There's nowhere open."

Bernard knew deep down what he was saying was true, but he still wasn't ready to hear it spelt out so starkly.

"Thanks a bunch. You certainly know how to cheer a chap up, don't you?"

"What are friends for?"

"I was being sarcastic!"

"Sarcasm is the lowest form of wit, don't you know? But speaking of friends, you couldn't cash me a cheque could you, old pal?"

"Again? How much for this time?"

"Oh, only for a piffling score, old man. We'll need to juice up the battle wagon to get down there."

"It doesn't cost that much to fill up a car, even a gas-guzzling monster like this. How much is four-star these days, 35p a gallon or thereabouts?"

"I do have other expenses my boy, other expenses."

Ronnie's eyes widened as Bernard reached into his pocket and pulled out a decent wad of notes.

"Sure you wouldn't prefer fifty? Twenty barely touches the sides with you."

"Tell you what, how about we make it a nice round hundred, save bothering you again this week."

Bernard dutifully handed over the money.

"Here you go."

"Splendid. I'll write you the cheque later, it's at the bottom of one of these bags. Speaking of which, could I chuck these in yours for a couple of days?"

For the first time, Bernard noticed the two pieces of luggage that Ronnie had dumped just out of sight to the left of the front door. One was a large holdall, the other wasn't a bag at all, but a suitcase.

"What have you got there?"

"All my worldly belongings. I'm having my flat redecorated this weekend. It's all being done out in Regency, and I don't want my hand-dedicated photo from Gielgud getting spattered in Etruscan Blue, do I?"

"OK, just dump them in the hall."

It seemed that Bernard had bought Ronnie's story, much to the older man's relief. Just as well. He didn't want to admit that he'd been unceremoniously kicked out of his flat and had spent the night sleeping in the car.

Bernard opened the front door and waited for Ronnie to put the bags in, but he didn't move. Instead, he just looked expectantly at his friend.

"Do the honours, old bean. I don't want to risk the old back, not with a couple of potential action roles coming up."

"Fine," said Bernard, annoyed at how he always seemed to be subservient to Ronnie, whatever they were doing.

He placed the bags inside, pulled out a small bag of his own and placed it on the back seat of the car.

"Wait here a moment," said Bernard. "I haven't had a wash or anything yet. You got me out of bed."

"You don't look as if you've had one all weekend, my boy. You need to get your act together. If you're going to become a lord of the manor, you'll need to look the part."

Bernard went back inside, cleaned himself up, and then re-emerged a few minutes later to find Ronnie back at the wheel, where he had again been blasting impatiently on the horn.

Bernard looked across to Mrs Johnson's house to see the curtains twitching, and bent down to speak to Ronnie through the open passenger side window.

"Do you have to do that? I do live here, you know! What are the neighbours going to think of that racket on a Sunday morning?"

"Oh, they won't mind when they see it's a classy motor like this. Now then, shall we get going? I've got the bubbly on ice on the back seat. Hop in."

He patted the passenger seat.

"You must be joking. You're not driving in that state, give me your keys."

"Capital idea. I drink, you drive. I like the way you think, Bernie boy!"

Ronnie got out and walked around to the passenger side as Bernard got in and took the wheel. As soon as they were both seated, Ronnie took out a cigarette and his personalised Zippo lighter with 'RR' engraved upon it. Then he prepared to spark up, much to Bernard's consternation.

"Oh no, absolutely not! I'm not inhaling your Stuyvesants for the next three hours."

"God, what a bore you are! No wonder Diane walked out."

"Right. You know what. Sod you. That's enough. I'm staying here."

"A little levity, my boy, to brighten the mood. Goodness, you're so uptight. This trip is just what you need. A break from sitting on your fat arse mooning over the past."

Bernard wasn't impressed, but Ronnie was correct about something. He did need a break from the old routine.

"Maybe you're right."

"Of course I'm right. I'm always right. Now let's get going. Your destiny is calling."

Bernard started the car and they drove away with Ronnie drinking from a hip flask. As they turned the corner at the end of the street, another car, a vintage hearse, pulled out of a parking space and began to pursue them. Had Ronnie been looking back, he would have recognised Charlie and Ken, the two henchmen who had been accompanying the Colonel on Friday evening.

They made good time in the Jensen, despite a few worrying backfires from the exhaust.

"Don't you ever get this thing serviced?" asked Bernard.

"I've had a bit of a cash flow problem."

"Don't I know it!"

"And I don't use it that much. Not when I can get taxis on expenses."

"Well let's hope it doesn't break down. At least the roads are quiet."

They made good time, and before noon they had clocked up over a hundred miles already.

"You do realise I'm going out of my way, don't you, coming all this way on a Sunday," remarked Ronnie.

"How so?"

"Missing my regular Sunday pilgrimage to the local house of God, my boy."

"Really? I thought you weren't welcome at the church anymore after what happened at Easter."

"As I have explained on countless occasions, I was taking that chalice to have it professionally cleaned."

"If you say so."

"Anyway, the vicar knows what side his bread's buttered. Having a star attending must double the congregation, at the very least. It makes for a very healthy collection plate."

"Yes, and wasn't there an issue with that on the day you persuaded them to let you deliver a sermon?"

"An easy mistake to make, my boy. It's traditional to have a whip round for the artiste."

"I'm sure. Anyway, how did your meeting with Terrance go yesterday?"

"How do you know about that?"

"Oh, er, someone must have told me on Friday," said Bernard hurriedly.

Ronnie was fuming but decided to bluff it out. Had they all been talking about him behind his back? How else would Bernard have known?

"Famously. He's offered me a new twelve-month contract."

"Really? I thought they weren't giving out twelve-month contracts at present. That's what the strike tomorrow is about."

"Yes, but I'm a special case, being the patriarch of the show. Mind you, I'm not sure if I'll take it. I've got more offers coming in right now than I can shake a shitty stick at. I had my agent on just before I left offering me the juvenile lead in a musical at the Theatre Royal."

"Juvenile lead? At your age?"

"Yes. I'm not as old as you think, dear boy. I seem older because I have gravitas."

"You're an ass, alright. Will you take it?"

"I'm not sure as Cubby is still pursuing me about the James Bond gig, have I told you about that? Connery doesn't want to do it anymore."

"You may have mentioned it a dozen or so times. But I heard Roger Moore was being lined up for it."

"I find that hard to believe. Roger Moore is just a television actor. They wouldn't give it to him."

"Isn't that what you are?"

"TV is merely one facet of my vast portfolio. As you know, I've trod the boards with the finest in the land. I'm an obvious choice for Bond."

"So what's stopping you?"

"I am loyal to the fans of *Sladen Square*. And of course, to you, Bernard. You are a lost soul in need of my support. I can't go flying off all over the world for months at a time having sex with beautiful women and leaving you on your own, can I?"

"I'm sure I'd cope without you."

"That's what my fourth wife said, and we all know what happened to her."

"Is that the one who fell down the stairs?"

"No, that was Monique, my third wife. My fourth wife was the one that decided she was a lesbian and ran off to America to join that weird religious cult."

"Sounds like she's coping quite well to me."

"That depends on your definition of coping."

"How many times have you been married, again?"

"Five times, my boy, five times. Every one a success. Listen, pull over, would you? I need to siphon the python."

Bernard pulled over into a small layby on the single-carriageway road which was taking them south toward Shroudshire. A few hundred yards behind, Charlie saw them stop and slowed right down, not wishing to be spotted.

"What do you think they're up to?" asked Ken, who was sitting alongside him.

"I don't know, but we need to check in with the boss. I had no idea we'd be coming this far."

"I saw a phone box a mile or so back. We could have used that."

"Then we'd have lost them, you idiot. We'll keep following until they get to wherever they're going, then we'll find a phone and report back."

Back up ahead, Ronnie had finished watering the stinging nettles and got back into the car, allowing them to get moving again. Much to Ronnie's irritation, Bernard had reverted to moping over Diane again.

"I can't help but think if only I had done things differently, we'd still be together now."

"Oh, give it a rest, Bernard. Do you know how pathetic you sound? Surely even someone as repugnant as you can find another woman."

"I don't want any other woman. She's the one. Once you've found the one, you never want another."

"Idealistic twaddle. I thought that about my first wife, Mildred, and look how that turned out."

"She caught you in bed with the bridesmaid on your wedding day!"

"I was drunk. They were both wearing white. It was a mistake anyone could have made."

The road took a bend to the right, bringing into view a sign which read 'Welcome to Shroudshire'.

"Ah good, we're almost there," remarked Ronnie. "Might just make closing time at this rate."

"Is that all you care about?"

"I never miss a drink at the pub on Sunday lunchtime. I want one, and I want it now. I find that if I pursue what I want everything else just falls into place. Rathbone rule number one."

"Yeah, you certainly look after number one alright."

"As should you, dear boy. You would be far happier if you adhered to the Rathbone Rules. Do you still have the list I gave to you?"

"No, I think they are at home somewhere," said Bernard, not wanting to admit he had burnt them, along with Diane's things, the previous day.

"Ah, you see. There is your problem. You must read them. Read, absorb, and prosper. The rules have helped me become the success I am today."

"Yeah, the man who's too big for James Bond!" replied Bernard sarcastically. As was frequently the case, his humour was lost on Ronnie who continued, unperturbed.

"I believe that rule seven would be of the most utility to you in this situation – make yourself happy and sod everybody else."

"But Diane is the one who made me happy, the only one. She always was."

"No, she wasn't. Look, I remember the real story. You were always complaining about her. She was always complaining about you."

"Yes, but since she's walked out, I realise that I was in the wrong and she was in the right. You see…"

"Ah, now I'm going to have to stop you there and refer you to rule fourteen. When someone walks out of your life, you let them go. Also, rule eleven: I am always right."

"It's easy for you, though isn't it? You don't have a heart or a conscience. You're alright. But I do and I'm not alright. Sometimes I think I'll never be alright again. And nothing you're saying is making things any better. If anything, you're making it worse."

He glanced down at the petrol gauge. They had filled up not long after they left, but this thing was exceptionally thirsty. They were down to half a tank already.

When he looked back up, he was in for a shock. Standing in the road, right in front of him was a hooded figure in a cloak, carrying a scythe. It was extending an arm towards him, revealing a bony hand and a skeletal finger, gesturing to Bernard to come towards him.

Nobody could have failed to recognise the identity of the thing in front of him. Everyone had heard of the Grim Reaper and now here he was. Had he come for him? Was he to die here, right now, perhaps in some sort of road traffic accident? Perhaps it was for the best. He had already decided that life wasn't worth living without Diane.

All these thoughts took barely a second before instinct kicked in and he slammed on the brakes.

Chapter Three
June 1972

"What the bloody hell do you think you're doing, you great oaf!" exclaimed Ronnie!

Just before Bernard's emergency stop, he had been taking a swig from his hip flask. Now half the contents of the flask were distributed all down his front, staining his tie and his waistcoat. In addition, the ice bucket in the back had flown off the seat, smashing the bottle of champagne and sending ice cubes flying up into the air and all over the back of Ronnie's head.

It wasn't so much the clothes he was worried about, though, more the loss of his beloved brandy and the celebratory champagne he had been saving for later.

"You've made me spill five shillings of perfectly good pop down my tweeds! And the bubbly's gone for a burton!"

"Didn't you see it?" said Bernard, in a panicked tone. His face had gone rather pale at the horrific image that was now etched firmly in his mind.

The Jensen had skidded and come to a complete stop, after swerving into the middle of the road where it was now straddling the white line at a forty-five-degree angle to the road.

Fortunately, nothing was coming towards them and they hadn't been shunted in the rear either. The only car behind was the hearse that was trailing them and they were a good quarter of a mile behind. Had either looked back, they might have questioned why it too had stopped but

Ronnie was too busy wiping down his front with a blue silk handkerchief. This too was engraved with his initials.

Bernard, meanwhile, was scanning the road, trying to spot the terrifying figure of the Reaper. It had appeared exactly as he had seen it portrayed in the countless old horror films that he had seen. But the road ahead was empty.

"See what?" asked Ronnie.

"The figure! In the road!"

"I saw nothing."

"Well, I saw it, clear as day. Perhaps I hit it."

Bernard got out of the car, bent down and looked underneath. There was nothing there, and he got back into the car, as Ronnie looked on disapprovingly.

"I worry about your state of mind, dear boy, I really do. Imagining things that aren't there, indeed. Are you still taking those happy pills the doctor gave you? They could be causing you to hallucinate. Perhaps I ought to take over the driving for a bit."

"No, thank you very much. You must have nailed half a bottle of brandy on the way here, plus what you had at breakfast. If anyone should be seeing things, it's you."

"Some of us can handle it, dear boy. Others cannot. That's why I can still enjoy liquor, and you can't."

"You don't have to keep reminding me," said Bernard, annoyed at Ronnie's constant digs.

He restarted the engine and pulled away again, followed by the hearse at a discreet distance. Ronnie fell silent for the moment as he continued his clean-up operation, leaving Bernard to brood on the situation. There was no denying it, Ronnie was a bloody liability. He claimed to be a friend but all he ever brought was trouble. Add to that the constant belittling, and he did wonder why he had bothered to bring him along. It was time he said something.

"You're a bit of a wanker, aren't you, Ronnie?"

"You have no proof for such a vile accusation."

"What about when Verity caught you in your dressing room?"

"Unsubstantiated nonsense. As I said at the time, the dressers had placed too much talcum powder in my costume."

"You were naked!"

"I had to disrobe; the itching was too great. Anyway, let's get a shift on. We're going to miss last orders at this rate."

Bernard couldn't be bothered to respond. What was the point of trying to have a sensible conversation with a man who never took anything seriously?

"Look! It's that way," called out Ronnie. "Slow down or you'll miss the turn."

Ronnie pointed to a small sign pointing to the right, about twenty yards ahead, which informed them that Weirdwell was just three miles away. They turned into a narrow country lane and began to negotiate their way around the tight twists and turns. It was a single-track road with passing places, but they didn't encounter a single car on the way.

Ken and Charlie followed but stayed completely out of sight. It was one thing tailing the Jensen on the main road, but it would have looked very suspicious if they had been spotted in the rear-view mirror here.

Three miles seemed to take an age on the narrow road, but eventually they emerged into the outskirts of a pretty quintessential English village. Weirdwell was a small place and it was but a short drive to the triangular-shaped green in the centre of the village. The green was bordered by a church on one side, some village stores on another, and a traditional country pub named The Five Stones on the third. All the buildings in the square had thatched rooves, and the traditional scene was completed by a red pillar box and matching phone box outside the stores.

They appeared to have arrived during some sort of event. All the buildings were festooned with bunting and balloons and the green was a hive of activity where the villagers had set up stalls and tents, as crowds of happy children ran around. There was also what looked suspiciously to Ronnie like a group of Morris dancers in the middle of the green. He wasn't a fan.

"It looks like there's some sort of festival going on," said Bernard.

"Perhaps they heard I was coming, and set this all up in my honour," suggested Ronnie.

"Hardly. It's probably just the annual village fete or something."

"How ghastly. Some old spinsters from the local Women's Institute with their homemade cakes, old gits showing off their revolting marrows from their allotments, and everyone else fobbing off their old tat in what amounts to a glorified jumble sale. I wouldn't be seen dead at such a gathering. And even worse, there are some Morris dancers over there. Appalling."

"I should keep your head down, then. What with you being so famous, they'll probably try and get you to carry out the official opening."

There were several trucks decked out as floats around the green, presumably for some sort of procession, but Bernard managed to find a parking place directly in front of the pub. This was much to Ronnie's approval, and he took out his pocket watch as the car glided to a halt.

"Good, it's only a quarter to. There's still time to get a couple of liveners in."

"I'll see you in there. I'm desperate for the lavvy. Unlike you, I managed to refrain from urinating in public on the way here. Order me a lemonade or something."

Bernard headed for a small brick outbuilding with a corrugated iron roof to the side of the pub. The word Gents was crudely chalked on the door. Ronnie, on the other hand, made a beeline straight for the front door. Had he stopped to look around him, he might have appreciated the wisteria that spread across the front of the whitewashed building, but he had eyes only for his next drink.

As they disappeared through their respective doorways, Charlie and Ken's hearse arrived in the village centre, parking up next to the red telephone box across the green from the pub. Charlie got out of the car, twopence piece in hand, stepped into the phone box, and dialled.

Back in Manchester, the Colonel was relaxing in his luxury penthouse flat in his silk Japanese dressing gown when the telephone rang. Sunday was a day of leisure and pleasure for him. There was no racing or football on the Sabbath which gave him a day off from running his betting empire. He also didn't believe in maiming people on a Sunday. He wasn't a particularly religious man but still felt that God wouldn't approve. As a last resort, if a beating was unavoidable, he had Charlie and Ken do the dirty work on his behalf.

"Hello, Berman's Dry Cleaning?" enquired the Colonel. This was his standard procedure when answering the phone until he knew who was calling. He did own a dry cleaner's shop that went by that name, but it didn't do much in the way of cleaning. He had acquired it from the previous owner to settle a gambling debt shortly before said owner's mysterious disappearance. The main thing it laundered these days was money.

"It's me, boss," said Charlie, on the other end.

"Ah, good afternoon, Charles, how's it all going? Are you still keeping tabs on Ronnie, as per my instructions?"

"We certainly are. If you ask me, he's up to something. He went to pick up his little friend, and now they've driven halfway across the country to some village in the middle of nowhere in Shroudshire."

"Shroudshire, eh? Fascinating. That's somewhere down Cheltenham way, isn't it? I used to know a racehorse trainer in that neck of the woods. Client of mine. Nice chap. Such a shame what happened to him after that little bit of business we had at Uttoxeter went awry."

"What's the plan now then? Do you want us to do him over?"

"No, no, Charlie, we aren't savages. We have a gentlemen's agreement. He's got until Friday to pay, and I'm intrigued as to where he thinks he's going to conjure up the money. My gut instinct tells me this little jaunt he's gone on is something to do with it. If he does magic up some money, I want to know where it came from, for future reference. If he doesn't, then you can do him over, to use your charming vernacular, on Friday."

"Right you are, boss."

"Good, well keep a close eye on them and report back to me when you can. Not too late, mind, I'm entertaining this evening."

With that, the Colonel hung up and Charlie returned to the car. There was nothing for him and Ken to do now but keep an eye on Ronnie's car and wait.

While Charlie had been on the phone, Ronnie had been acquainting himself with the owners of the pub. He had wasted no time striding up to the bar to order a drink from the middle-aged redhead behind the bar, elbowing a couple of elderly locals out of the way as he went.

"Good afternoon, and may I say what a magnificent hostelry you have here, madam."

The woman looked open-mouthed at Ronnie, a look he had seen many times before. It was a look of recognition, which was good news. Any opportunity to use his celebrity status to his advantage was always to be welcomed. This was one of the great things about being famous. People knew who you were, and you didn't need to know who they were, because, well, they were irrelevant, weren't they?

"Oh, my, you're Ronald Rathbone aren't you?"

"Yes, I rather think I am!"

"My name's Brenda and I'm the landlady here. I'm a huge fan of *Sladen Square*. You must let me buy you a drink. How about a pint of our local ale, Fendara's Ruin?"

Ronnie was in his element. She was both starstruck, and in the happy position of dispensing the drinks. It was a shame it was nearly closing time, but never mind, he would try to make the most of it.

"I'd prefer a large brandy if it's all the same with you."

"A pleasure," replied Brenda as she turned to pour a double from the optics.

"Marvellous," replied Ronnie.

"I remember you saying you drank brandy in that profile *TV Times* did of you," she added, as she turned back to him.

"Common rag!" exclaimed Ronnie, who disapproved of the *TV Times*. Despite *Sladen Square* being an ITV show, he still considered it to be a channel for the lower orders. People of sophistication such as himself watched the BBC and read the *Radio Times*.

"I beg your pardon?" she said, looking at him somewhat perturbed.

"Oh, er I was just noticing some festivities on the common out there. Rather like rag week at Oxford. Quiet in here, though."

It wasn't a particularly convincing bit of backtracking for his little outburst, but it seemed to work. To him, she was just some irksome local, but it would pay to keep her sweet to keep the drinks flowing.

"We're normally busier than this on a Sunday lunchtime, but most of the village is busy getting ready for the festival."

"Festival, eh? So that's what's going on."

"Yes, it goes back to the old times. There used to be a stone circle near the village. One large slab, surrounded by five upright stones in the shape of a pentagram. That's how the pub got its name."

"Used to be?"

"Yes. It mysteriously disappeared sometime in the Middle Ages. There are depictions of it everywhere, but of the stones, not a sign. No one is even sure where they are, now. They were bluestones, the same as the ones used at Stonehenge, so not particularly easy to move. There are all sorts of theories about what happened to them."

A slight, balding man with grey hair swept across his forehead in the style of Bobby Charlton, emerged from a door behind the bar. He was carrying a crate of Schweppes tonic bottles and it looked like hard work, as he was sweating slightly and out of breath. He plonked them down on the bar, making the bottles rattle, alerting Brenda to his presence.

"We've got a visitor, Alan, look who it is," she said.

Alan looked Ronnie up and down, but there wasn't a hint of recognition.

"Who's he?" asked Alan, delivered in a tone that Ronnie considered to be rather rude.

"It's Ronald Rathbone, star of stage and screen!"

"Never heard of him. Is he here to open the fete?"

"Hardly. I can't imagine the bumpkins in this little backwater being able to afford my fee," remarked Ronnie, without realising that he had just insulted the entire village, including his hosts. Brenda looked annoyed, but fortunately for Ronnie, Bernard chose this moment to enter the pub.

As soon as Brenda clapped eyes on him, she shrieked in excitement.

"Look, Alan! It's Bernard Bradshaw!"

It was a far more enthusiastic response than she had given Ronnie. His irritation grew because having failed to recognise him, Alan clearly knew who Bernard was right away.

"Barrel of Laughs Bradshaw!" exclaimed Alan. "Ey up!"

"Ey up!" repeated Brenda, causing Ronnie to roll his eyes in frustration. People up and down the land had been repeating this bloody catchphrase ever since Bernard had flogged it to death in a godawful sitcom he had made for Yorkshire Television.

"A common catchphrase if you ask me," remarked Ronnie. "Still, I imagine it's pitched at about the right level of intellect for *TV Times* readers."

"Er, yeah! Ey up to you too!" said Bernard, playing up to his newfound fans.

"Bernard, this is such an honour. To have such a star, here in our pub!" said Alan.

"Unbelievable!" declared Ronnie. "And what about me?"

"We were such big fans of *Stop Mithering Me*," remarked Brenda. "Will you be making more?"

"Funnily enough there is some talk of making another series, fingers crossed," replied Bernard.

"That would be wonderful," said Brenda. "Now, Bernard, I have to ask, but is it true what I read in the *News of the World* about you and Diane?"

"Oh, heavens above, woman," said Ronnie. "I've been trying to keep his mind off that, and now you're going to set him off again."

"Yes, I'm afraid so. She's the only woman I've ever truly loved," said Bernard.

Ronnie wasn't in the mood to hear Bernard pouring out his life story to Brenda. He exaggeratedly cleared his throat, got hold of his pocket watch and tapped it. He had already knocked back the double brandy Brenda had given him on the house.

"Is there any chance of getting another drink around here? It's not two o'clock yet."

Brenda shot him a less-than-friendly look. Her demeanour had gone from warm and welcoming when Ronnie had first come in to decidedly frosty. A few minutes in Ronnie's company had that effect on a lot of women.

"Yes, but you'll have to pay for this one. Don't you worry though, Bernard, yours is on the house. I can see you've been through a tough time. Have you been eating properly? I can knock you up something to eat if you like."

"I say, this is quite ridiculous," said Ronnie crossly. "He's only broken up with his wife, it's not like it's the end of the world. He just needs to get himself another one. Like I usually do."

Brenda had seen and heard enough of Ronnie now to make her mind up about him.

"You know, I'm beginning to think that what Diana Dors said about you on *Parkinson* was right. You are a horrible man."

"You wouldn't think that if you were in my shoes. I've had to put up with months of listening to this rubbish. But fine, I'll pay for my own drink. Or rather he will. Get your wallet out, Bernard."

"Umm, no, I don't think so. I'm getting a bit fed up with you taking advantage of me. You can pay for it out of the hundred I gave you this morning. And I'll have a lemonade, please."

"Good for you," said Brenda, turning to get the drinks. "Don't let him lord it over you."

Ronnie threw a look of disgust in her direction before Alan piped up again.

"So what brings you here, Bernard? Surely, you've not come all this way for our little festival?"

"No, I'm here for the reading of my late Uncle Arthur's will, not that I've ever met him."

"Arthur? Not old Arthur Blackwood up at Fendara's Lodge? The late Lord Blackwood?"

"Yeah, that was him."

Ronnie was all ears, keen to hear more about Bernard's mysterious late relative. On the one hand, he hated the idea of Bernard inheriting a title. But on the other, it could be very lucrative.

Alan's response to Bernard's confirmation was an unexpected one. His jovial manner vanished, and he abruptly changed the subject.

"My goodness, it's after two. I need to ring for time."

He reached up to an ornate copper bell over the bar and rang it enthusiastically.

"Time, gentlemen, please."

And with that, he promptly disappeared back through the door whence he had originally come. His sudden departure hadn't gone unnoticed, leaving Bernard scratching his metaphorical head wondering what on earth he had said wrong. Usually, it was Ronnie who put his foot in it, but he hadn't said anything since the altercation over who was paying for the drinks.

"What was all that about?" he asked Brenda.

"Oh, nothing, it's just… well, he was a very odd man, your Uncle Arthur," explained Brenda.

"Now there's a surprise!" interjected Ronnie, in between swigs of his latest brandy.

"In what way?" asked Bernard, as Alan returned to the bar carrying another crate, this time containing bottles of Cresta soft drinks.

"Well, eccentric like. There were always rumours about mysterious, ghostly figures at the house. The most well-known is that of a strange creature in a hooded cloak, appearing from nowhere, and then vanishing. Many say it was Arthur, dressed up. But others claim it was Death, the Grim Reaper himself."

"Now that is interesting," said Bernard. "I saw a figure in a hooded cloak on the way here who looked like Death."

"You mean, you thought you saw," said Ronnie. "I suggest you pay no attention, woman, the poor boy's seeing things. Come along, Bernard, it is time to go. The will is being read at three. Alan, Brenda, I would like to say that it has been a pleasure. But as we all know that would be a damned lie."

"Oh well, must go," said Bernard reluctantly. "Nice to meet you both, will no doubt see you again later."

"Come in any time you like," said Brenda. "But, Ronnie? You're barred."

"Like I care," remarked Ronnie as he made his way to the door.

Back outside, the sun had come out from behind the clouds. Ronnie reached into his breast pocket and pulled out a pair of sunglasses whilst Bernard took out the telegram to check the address of the solicitors. Navigation wasn't his strong point, so he handed it to Ronnie who quickly removed his sunglasses again, taking out his pince-nez instead.

After a moment examining it, he pointed to a small lane along the side of the village stores. Then Ronnie briefly returned to the Jensen, and unseen by Bernard, grabbed something from beneath the back seat which he stuffed into his pocket. After that he replaced his sunglasses.

They began to make their way across the green where the festivities were now in full flow. Plenty of people recognised Bernard and stopped him for autographs, but Ronnie was largely ignored. Bernard even got a chaste kiss on the cheek from a lovely young lady who was dressed up as the carnival queen. She didn't give Ronnie a second look and he was forced to content himself with occasionally muttering words like 'peasants', 'oiks' and 'bumpkins' under his breath until they got through the crowd.

Eventually they reached the far side of the green, taking them close to the hearse. Alarmed by their approach, Charlie and Ken sank as low as they could in their seats, but they had nothing to worry about. Bernard and Ronnie were too focused on finding their way to their destination to pay any attention.

Just around the corner they found the solicitor's office, which was another vintage thatched building, this one dating from the Tudor era, judging by the black beams on the white exterior. Walking up the steps, past numerous rose bushes resplendent with flowers, they went in through a low wooden door that looked as if it had been there since the house was built. Being six feet tall, Ronnie had to duck down to get through.

The door led into a reception area, where a slim young lady was sitting behind an oak desk. She sported a blonde beehive hairdo that reminded Bernard of Brigitte Bardot. As they entered, she looked up from the Hermes 3000 typewriter she had been tapping away on and smiled.

"Good afternoon. Can I help you?"

Ronnie made no effort to disguise his interest in the young woman, despite being more than twice her age. He removed his sunglasses again and put on his usual charm.

"Hello, my dear, don't alert the press, but I am Ronald Rathbone and I am here to safely deliver Bernard Bradshaw esquire into your safe custody for the reading of his late uncle's will."

"Ah, yes, I'll let Mr Underhill know you are here."

She jumped up lithely from the desk and made her way into the office behind her, giving the lascivious Ronnie a full view of her rear. He was about to comment, but Bernard hastily intervened.

"Put your tongue away, Ronnie," said Bernard, disapprovingly. "I know what you're thinking. You were about to start perving over her like some dirty old man."

"There's nothing wrong with appreciating the female form, dear boy. If we didn't, humans would go extinct."

"It's the way you appreciate it that worries me. Now, changing the subject, I hope all this is going to be worth it after you talked me into driving all this way."

"It's sure to be. You heard what that bald git of a landlord said. He confirmed that old Arthur was indeed a lord. That means he must have had bags of money. Why else would this Mr Underhill open up shop on a Sunday? Places like this never open on a Sunday. There must be some lucre in it for them."

"I suppose so."

"There is no suppose about it. I know what solicitors are like. They made a fortune out of me every time I got divorced. Good job yours came through a few weeks ago really, wasn't it? Otherwise, Diane would have been entitled to half of all this, you know."

"And I would gladly give it to her."

"Of course, you would. Rationality has never been your strong point."

Ronnie reached into his pocket and pulled out his hip flask.

"I thought you'd emptied that on the way here?" said Bernard.

"I had another one stuffed under the back seat. See? The other one was red, and this one's blue. I took the opportunity of retrieving it after we left the pub. Rule number six. Never be out of reach of a drink."

Before Ronnie could unscrew the top, the receptionist returned to usher them in.

"You can go through now, Mr Bradshaw. Will your friend be joining you?"

"No, I…"

"I shall indeed, mademoiselle," interrupted Ronnie. "My place is by your side, remember?"

"Very well," said Bernard. "But put that flask away. We don't want to create the wrong impression."

Reluctantly, Ronnie complied, as the young woman held the door open for them. He took the opportunity to wink at her on the way past when Bernard wasn't looking, and she didn't look impressed.

In the office, Mr Underhill was seated behind a large mahogany desk, more impressive than the one in reception as befitted his status. As Bernard and Ronnie entered he got to his feet to greet them.

"Ah, Mr Bradshaw. Do sit down. A pleasure to meet you. My wife and I are great fans of your work. And who is this? Your chauffeur?"

"How dare you, you jumped up little clerk! I am Ronald Rathbone, once nominated for best actor!"

"For an Oscar?" enquired the solicitor.

"No, it was for the Newton-le-Willows amateur dramatics society," said Bernard.

"Rathbone? Ah yes, I remember. The man who dropped his trousers in front of the Queen. Sit down, won't you both? Now then, firstly I'd like to say how very sorry I am for your loss, Mr Bradshaw."

"That's alright, I never met him, Mr Underhill."

"Call me Gerald."

"I had never even heard of him until the telegram arrived, Gerald."

"Well, as your uncle's sole living relative it took us some time to track you down, Bernard. You see your mother left the family home back in the 1920s when she ran away with your father. This was due to her father, old Mr Blackwood, greatly disapproving of their liaison."

"This is all news to me. I knew my mam came from a posh background because she didn't speak like the other women on the estate. But she never spoke about her family."

"Nor they, her, after she had left. Anyway, that's ancient history now. Shall we just crack on with it?"

"If we could," said Ronnie impatiently, tapping his fingers repeatedly on the desk, much to Gerald's annoyance.

"Thank you, yes, please carry on," said Bernard.

"Here we go then," said Gerald, ceremoniously running the edge of a small dagger along the gold seal which lined the edge of the envelope. He pulled out the document, which was handwritten on a faded yellow parchment, and began to read:

"I, Arthur Blackwood, being of sound mind and body, hereby leave to my sole nephew, Bernard, my home, Fendara's Lodge, and all my worldly goods and belongings."

"Is that it?" asked Ronnie. "No large sums of cash? Swiss bank accounts?"

"No, the deceased left only a token amount of cash. You see, the Blackwoods were a family who was land rich, but had very little use for money."

"This is an outrage! My friend has come a long way for this, even jeopardising his last chance with the love of his life. Bernard, I told you, you should have gone around with those flowers this morning."

"You said nothing of the sort, Ronnie. Anyway, I can't understand what you are so upset about. The house must be worth a fortune."

"That's no good to me today, though, is it? Unless the old git had anything valuable lying around in the house, we may as well go home."

"Is there anything?" asked Bernard. "Can we go up there and take a look?"

"It appears that there is," replied Gerald, turning to the second page of the document.

"Ahh! Here we go," said Ronnie. "I knew the old git would have something squirrelled away for a rainy day."

"As a condition of the will you must be in the house at the stroke of midnight on the day that follows Midsummer's day. Good Lord, that's today. That explains why the conditions of the will stipulated that it must be read on this date and at this time. It's not ideal, you know. I'm having to pay Sally double to come in on a Sunday. I shall have to reflect this in my fee."

"I knew it," said Ronnie.

"A night in a haunted house? A bit of a cliché, isn't it?" said Bernard.

"He never said it was haunted," said Ronnie. "It was you that said that. So, is that all we need to do? Stay there for one night? That doesn't sound like too much of an imposition, does it? I mean we've come all this way, may as well make the most of it. And we don't have to work tomorrow because they're all on strike."

"What's the place like?" asked Bernard.

"Oh, it's a fine house. Built just before the Civil War. Your uncle was quite the collector and the place is stuffed with the finest collection of vintage wines and antiques this side of the Cotswolds."

"Splendid! That's more like it!" said Ronnie excitedly. "We would be delighted to accept your deal."

"The offer is not yours to accept, Mr Rathbone. It is up to Mr Bradshaw here to decide."

"Come on, Bernard. It's an offer you can't refuse."

"Very well."

"Excellent," said Gerald. "I shall ring Jamset at the house and tell him to expect your arrival.

"Who's Jamset?" asked Ronnie.

"He is the butler and has been left in charge since Lord Blackwood's death. He will assist you with anything you need."

"Our own personal butler, eh?" said Ronnie. "This gets better and better."

"That's all settled then," said Gerald. "I suggest you speak to Sally on the way out and she will give you directions."

"Thank you," said Bernard. "Best we be on our way, then."

"It's been a pleasure to meet you, Bernard, and if I may be so bold, may I say 'ey up'!"

Gerald offered his hand to Bernard who shook it vigorously, before saying, "Ey up," in return.

Ronnie then held out his hand, but Gerald seemingly didn't notice and held the door for them instead, ushering them back into the reception area.

"Rude!" exclaimed Ronnie.

Back in reception, Bernard turned to Sally.

"Hello again. Would you be kind enough to give us directions to Fendara's Lodge?"

"Of course, it's very straightforward. Here, let me sketch you a quick map."

She began to draw on an expensive-looking embossed sheet of paper, as Bernard looked on. Ronnie, meanwhile, couldn't resist chancing his arm.

"Do you fancy a night in a country house, my dear? Fine wines, scintillating company."

"If you mean in Fendara's Lodge, no way! The number of stories I've heard about that place!"

"Fear not, sweet flower. You'll have me to protect you."

"Leave her alone, Ronnie," said Bernard. "She's young enough to be your daughter."

"There's a thought. She may very well be. I toured *Blithe Spirit* down here with Rex Harrison back in the early fifties. Things got rather lively with some of the local ladies, I can tell you. These country folk aren't as shy as they let on."

Ignoring Ronnie, Sally showed Bernard where to go on the map.

"So straight up here, and then right at the top of the hill."

"Thank you, Sally. You have been very helpful."

Bernard made his way to the door, followed by Ronnie, who was disappointed at Sally's lack of interest. What was he doing wrong? Why didn't women fancy him anymore? He was charming, sophisticated, and a star. It was becoming incredibly frustrating. Never mind, there was still the inheritance. He had to make getting his hands on that the priority.

On the way back to the car, they wisely avoided the crowds on the village green and walked along a public footpath that took them through the churchyard instead. It wasn't very well kept, with weeds everywhere and a lot of overhanging trees. The sun had also gone in and it had turned inexplicably cold. It all combined to make Bernard nervous. He couldn't quite put his finger on it, but something was making him feel distinctly uneasy.

"I'm not sure about all this, you know. All night stuck in some strange house with nothing to do."

"Nonsense. It will be fun. Country house, a cellar full of wine. What could possibly go wrong?"

As Ronnie was speaking, Bernard cast a glance around the churchyard. Then he spotted a figure right over the other side, about a hundred yards away, looking directly at him. It was the same hooded figure he had seen on the road earlier.

"Ronnie! It's that hooded stranger again from earlier! Look!"

He'd had time to think since the previous encounter, and had concluded that it couldn't have been the Grim

Reaper. That was silly. Perhaps it was just someone dressed up for the celebrations who had got lost on the way to Weirdwell. Well, he was here now, so he could ask him. He was determined to clear up the mystery and began to run across the churchyard. Ronnie, exasperated, called after him.

"I can't see anything. Where are you going? Honestly, you are a right royal pain in the arse."

Bernard could still see the hooded figure, standing directly behind a freshly filled in grave. It was carrying the scythe which was usually associated with the Grim Reaper. It was probably just a fancy dress prop, but why dress up as Death for a summer festival? Surely, that was more of a Halloween thing.

He ran towards it, but as he approached the gravestone he was startled by a murder of crows. They flew out of an old elm tree, squawking all around him, before flying off towards the church tower. By the time he focused his attention back on the gravestone, the strange figure had vanished.

He stopped when he reached the grave and waited for Ronnie to catch up, before turning to him to explain.

"I saw that hooded figure again. I thought at first it was someone in fancy dress, but then he just vanished. Do you think it could be the ghost of my uncle? Brenda said something about him dressing up like the Grim Reaper."

"Hahaha! Have you taken leave of your senses, man? I think sobriety is sending you mad."

"No, look. This is the exact spot where it disappeared. It's Arthur's grave."

"It didn't disappear because it was never there. It was a mere apparition brought on by your hysterical mental state."

"I don't care what you say. It was definitely there."

"Alright, whatever you say. It's a shame they've buried the old man already. You're not going to get hold of those gold teeth now. Still, if what Underhill said was true, there are all sorts of other goodies waiting at the house. Now can we please get on?"

Bernard was feeling increasingly uneasy, but they had come this far, it seemed pointless not seeing it through now. They walked through to the front gate of the churchyard and back into the village centre. It didn't escape Bernard's notice that as soon as they were out of the churchyard the sun came back out and the air was again filled with the warmth of the summer's day they had been enjoying earlier.

They worked their way around the edge of the green, managing to avoid any more autograph hunters. Once they were back in the car, Bernard reversed out and they began to make their way up to the house, with Ronnie giving directions from the map that Sally had given them.

Sticking to their instructions, Charlie and Ken followed.

Chapter Four
June 1972

It was only about a mile to the grounds of the Blackwood estate, the entrance to which was through an open pair of tall wrought iron gates. These were bordered on both sides by large wooden pillars carved with several rather sinister-looking gargoyles. It was an impressive sight which raised expectations as to just how grand this house was going to be. Even so, when they reached the end of the long gravel driveway flanked by mature leafy oaks, what they saw in front of them took their breath away.

Ronnie could scarcely believe his eyes at the size of the place. It looked like a stately home. It was set over three floors, and going by the number of windows must have had twenty bedrooms at least. There were turrets at both ends and a large castle-shaped tower in the centre with battlements at the top, suggesting that this building had been built with defence in mind.

In front of the house, the driveway split to form a large circle which surrounded a large garden area, laid mostly to lawn. It was decorated with several fountains and statues. Ronnie's first impression was that it reeked of wealth. However, it quickly became apparent that the estate was not being maintained in the manner it had been in the past. There were tell-tale signs everywhere, from the lichen and bird mess all over the statues, the stagnant green water in the fountains, and the unkempt state of the lawn which was riddled with dandelions and other weeds.

As they approached the house, it was clear that it too had seen better days. Some of the masonry was crumbling in places, the wooden window frames were showing signs of rot and there was a large chunk of rock not far from the front door which they could see had fallen from the battlements above where there was a gap as if they had lost a tooth.

Ronnie, however, was willing to overlook these imperfections in his excitement.

"You've well and truly struck gold here, old chap. This place must be worth a fortune."

"Cost a fortune to fix up more like. Look at the state of it. It's falling apart."

"Oh, it's nothing a lick of paint won't fix. It reminds me of the country pad I took my second wife to on our honeymoon. She was a virgin on our wedding night, did I tell you? She wasn't so innocent after a night being ravished by the Rathbone, I can tell you."

"Yes, so you've said. About fifty times. Seriously, places like this are not a goldmine. They're a bloody liability. There are the death duties, for a start. That's been the ruin of many of the aristocracy over the past century or so. Places like this simply aren't viable anymore as private homes. Why do you think so many are being turned into tourist attractions?"

"There you go, then. Open a theme park."

"That sounds a bit like hard work to me."

"What about a zoo, then? Everyone loves a zoo. There are always options. Let me refer you to rule number twenty-nine. Always look on the sunny side."

"I'm trying, Ronnie."

"You are very trying, Bernard. Here I am, offering you the benefit of my years of wisdom and experience, yet all you do is pooh-pooh my suggestions."

Bernard pulled up close to the front door and they got out of the car and had a quick wander along the front of the house, marvelling at the size of the place. It seemed even bigger up close. As they strolled, Bernard noted a few other signs of disrepair, including a broken window on an upper floor.

After a few minutes, they walked up to the front doorway of the house. It was seriously impressive, resembling as it did the front door of a castle. It was set in an archway at least eight feet in height and made of thick solid oak, strengthened all over by diagonal bracing. Each of the crisscrossing slats was studded with solid iron nails. Even Ronnie, who was a tall man, felt rather in awe as he approached.

"I won't have to worry about banging my head on this doorframe. Not like that solicitor's office in town. Makes sense, though, doesn't it? The aristocracy that lived here would have been tall and proud like me. Whereas the short-arsed peasants in the village would have only needed a door fit for hobbits."

"I didn't know you'd read Tolkien," replied Bernard.

"I haven't. But I auditioned for a part in the BBC radio adaptation, years ago. My agent advised me to turn it down, though, as there were far more prestigious film roles in the offing. I think they gave it to Valentine Dyall in the end."

"I'm surprised at that because I thought you would have had the perfect face for radio."

"Very funny. Now, let us announce our presence!"

However, before they could knock the door was opened by an Asian man dressed in traditional Indian clothing. Ronnie wasted no time in introducing himself.

"Ahh, you must be Jamset. My name's Ronald Rathbone, and this is Bernard Bradshaw. I expect you've heard of me. I'm very big in the Punjab."

Jamset looked Bernard and Ronnie up and down, as if he was weighing them up, but didn't speak. This led Ronnie to jump to the hasty conclusion that because of the man's appearance, his English must be poor.

He turned to Bernard and said, "Best you leave the talking to me on this one. I toured India with Terry Scott in the late fifties and I know how to deal with these fellows."

He turned back to Jamset and spoke slowly and deliberately, adopting a mock Indian accent.

"Hello. Do you speak any English?"

Much to Ronnie's chagrin, the man's response was delivered in an accent that wouldn't have been out of place for a BBC newsreader of the 1950s.

"I speak perfect English, thank you. I have lived my entire life in England and was educated here at Harrow. Are you feeling alright? You appear to be speaking in a strange accent."

"No, he isn't alright," said Bernard. "He's been drinking all day. I do apologise for his ignorant behaviour."

"It's perfectly alright, Mr Bradshaw. I am aware of Mr Rathbone's reputation."

"I don't have a reputation!" protested Ronnie. "Unless it is one for being one of the world's most acclaimed stars of stage and screen, of course."

"You recognise us, then?" said Bernard.

"Clearly, sir. Mr Underhill informed me of your impending arrival. Would you care to follow me?"

Jamset led the way into the large hallway, which had a chequered black and white marble floor, and an impressive wide staircase leading upwards. Bernard was followed by a slightly sheepish Ronnie, who felt that he had somehow got the worst of the exchange.

"Impertinent fellow," he muttered, as Jamset led them through the hallway at the front of the house. As he looked around, his eyes were instantly drawn to some of the oil paintings on the wall. Ronnie didn't know as much as he claimed about a lot of things but he did have a smattering of knowledge about art and he knew an old master when he saw one.

Outside, Ken and Charlie had parked up outside the main gates. The two thugs couldn't risk taking the car any further so proceeded on foot. It was a couple of hundred yards to the edge of the front gardens. This was where the tree-lined avenue ended but there were woods on both sides.

They concealed themselves just inside the woods, where they could keep an eye on the house without being spotted, arriving just in time to see the encounter at the front door. Ken was now observing this through a pair of binoculars that were hanging on a cord around his neck. Charlie, however, could not see a great deal at the distance, such was the vastness of the estate and was becoming frustrated at Ken hogging the binoculars. He felt that he should have custodianship of them. He was senior to Ken in the Colonel's pecking order, after all.

"They're going inside," said Ken.

"I want to see! Give me the binoculars. It's my turn!"

Ken tried to move out of the way as Charlie attempted to wrench the binoculars away from him, almost strangling him with the cord in the process. The net result was that both ended up falling backwards into a pile of stinging nettles.

Back in the house, Jamset was giving Bernard and Ronnie a guided tour of the ground floor. Although it had an impressive history, packed as it was with valuable items, the decor looked as tired as the exterior. Some of the carpets were threadbare and there were damp patches on the walls in places, not to mention an impressive collection of cobwebs.

Jamset knew a great deal about the history of the house, summarising it all for them as they left the hallway, along a corridor that led towards the drawing room.

"The original house was built by Sir Thomas Blackwood in the seventeenth century and was defended by him against a Roundhead attack in the Civil War. Hence the battlements on the tower above the entrance hall. The house has been the Blackwood family seat ever since. Arthur was the tenth generation to take charge of the estate, and he took it over as a young man following the death of his father in combat in 1915. And this, gentlemen, is the drawing room, which retains its initial design to this day."

Bernard took a moment to look around the impressive room. Whoever had furnished it had not been short of money. The walls were panelled, solid oak, decorated at intervals by red drapes. On each wall were large paintings of distinguished-looking gentlemen, presumably former owners of the house. Each wall also held a large candelabra, though the most impressive lighting feature was the huge chandelier in the centre of the ceiling.

His eyes couldn't help but be drawn to the magnificent open fireplace at the end of the room, which was made of marble and decorated with intricate floral carvings. The mantelpiece above was filled with antiques, as were the various sideboards around the room. There was also a large grandfather clock.

The floor was solid wood, covered in places by various rugs, and the furniture looked very opulent – plush velvet red sofas and chairs. Bernard had no idea what period they were from, but they hadn't come from MFI, that was for sure.

It all reeked of wealth, but also neglect. Everything was showing signs of wear and tear.

"How long have you been here, Jamset?" asked Bernard.

"My great-grandfather returned with Lord Henry Blackwood from his time in India during the nineteenth century and my family have been here ever since."

"That would explain your impeccable English."

"Indeed. I think your friend over there was a little surprised by that before," said Jamset, gesturing at Ronnie who had wandered off to the other side of the spacious room.

"He does tend to jump to an awful lot of false assumptions. It's going to get him in serious trouble one of these days."

As Bernard and Jamset continued their conversation, Ronnie was examining some of the many antiques in the room. He studied each one closely, using a jeweller's glass which he had plucked from one of his many pockets. Then he wrote down their estimated value in his notebook, the one with the faked photograph of him and Laurence Olivier on the front.

Looking around to check the others weren't looking, he took the opportunity to pilfer a couple of small items, slipping them into his inside jacket pockets. It didn't look as though he was going to be able to get any cash out of this trip, but if he could steal and sell a few trinkets he ought to be able to put enough together to get the Colonel off his back.

There was also the small matter of his recent destitution. He could probably make up some excuse to sleep in Bernard's spare room for a few days but the sooner he got his own place again, the better.

Bernard wasn't going to notice anything going missing, how could he? They had only just arrived here. Jamset, on the other hand, could be a problem. He wasn't entirely sure how he fitted into all of this but he clearly knew this place inside out and probably lived here. Still, if anything was said, he could always try to blame him. Bloody servants, dishonest all of them. Happy with his little haul for the moment, he turned back to the others.

"What should we do now, Jamset?" asked Bernard.

"If you'd care to wait here in the drawing room, I'll send for some tea."

"You haven't got anything a little more medicinal, have you?" asked Ronnie, hopefully. "Drop of brandy or something?"

"I don't think we have any brandy, sir, but I believe that cook may have some cooking sherry, will that suffice?"

"Ah yes, nothing but the best in this house, eh?"

"Very good, sir. I shall attend to it."

Jamset left the room, leaving the two of them alone.

"No brandy, indeed," said Ronnie. "Are you seriously telling me an estate this size isn't packed to the rafters with the finest wines and spirits in the land? Surely, Bernard, your uncle must have had a well-stocked cellar for entertaining?"

"I don't know, perhaps he wasn't into all that," said Bernard. "You heard what they said at the pub about him, that he was a bit odd. Maybe he didn't do any entertaining."

"Yes, well, being odd probably runs in the family," said Ronnie, just as a large grandfather clock struck 6pm. He walked over to it, taking out his pocket watch as he went.

"I say, look at that, it's still keeping perfect time after all these years. Made by a proper craftsman, that was. And probably very valuable. Like almost everything else in this room."

Ronnie looked back to Bernard, who looked distracted. Had he even heard what he had just said? He wasn't pining over Diane again, was he? He had better bloody not be.

"I don't like this room," said Bernard. "It feels strange. Almost, kind of, like haunted."

"Never mind how it feels. It's a little goldmine!"

"You keep saying that, but I told you before, this place must cost a fortune to run. Not only the upkeep, but what about Jamset, and the cook? And any other staff they've got knocking about? I'm sure that big lawn out there doesn't cut itself."

"It doesn't look like it's been cut for a while if you ask me," replied Ronnie, casting his eye out of the window.

"Yes, well, the point is we don't know how many staff there are or what they do. But I do know who is going to be paying all their wages from now on. Me."

"Oh, they're only humble domestic staff. They earn a pittance, boy, a mere pittance. Sell a few of the things in here, and you'll be laughing."

Jamset returned to the room, carrying an ornate golden tea tray, containing what to Ronnie's trained eye looked like an extremely expensive set of Royal Doulton china.

"Your refreshments, gentlemen."

"Ah, tiffin. Good. No sherry?" asked Ronnie.

"I'm afraid not sir, cook used the last up some time ago."

Jamset placed the tray on an antique French coffee table. It had a white marble surface supported by ornately carved legs. On closer inspection, Ronnie could see they were gold-plated. At least that's what he assumed. They couldn't be solid gold, could they? Pound signs began to dance in front of his eyes once again.

At the exact moment Jamset put the tray down, Bernard gasped as he felt an icy chill rush through the air. It was just as if he had walked into an open freezer. He had already been feeling uneasy about this room and this had spooked him even further, especially as there was no evidence of anything that could have caused the sudden drop in temperature.

"What was that?" he exclaimed.

"What was what?" asked Ronnie, who was seemingly unaffected. Jamset, however, seemed to pick up on what Bernard was feeling.

"Are you cold, sir?" he said, looking at Bernard, who was now shivering. "Would you like me to fetch you a blanket?"

"In June?" asked Ronnie incredulously. "You'll be suggesting we light a fire next."

"No, it's alright," said Bernard, as in an instant the temperature around him returned to normal. "I just felt a chill for a moment, but it was very strange. It feels almost as if there's a presence in here. Like when you almost keep seeing things out of the corner of your eye but when you turn, there's nothing there. Can't you feel it, Ronnie?"

"Quite frankly? No."

Bernard cast his eye around the room to see if he could find a rational explanation. The window wasn't open, so it couldn't have come from outside, but why would it anyway? As Ronnie had rightly pointed out, it was a June day and a warm one at that. But something else next to the window did catch his eye.

"Look! That grandfather clock! It was over near the fireplace before. Now it's by the window!"

"Was it?" asked Ronnie.

"Yes! You're seriously telling me you don't remember? You walked over to the bloody thing. You were talking about it."

"Rule forty-eight, old china. Don't waste valuable grey matter on trivial details."

First, there had been the chill and then the mysterious moving clock. But they paled by comparison to what Bernard saw next. Once again, something in the corner of his eye caught his attention but this time when he turned around it was well and truly there. As he looked across the room he saw a book floating through the air by itself, towards a large bookshelf.

"Ronnie! Look at that!"

But he was too late. By the time Ronnie turned around the book had neatly slotted itself into a gap on the shelf. Jamset seemingly hadn't noticed either, as he was busy setting out cups and saucers on the table.

"Look at what?" said Ronnie. "Another of your non-existent apparitions? You've been doing this all day and it's becoming frightfully tiresome now."

"That book! It was moving by itself!"

Bernard walked over to the shelf and looked at the dusty old book, which was entitled *Eighteenth-Century British Colonialism*. It didn't look as if it had been moved for ages, and nor did anything else on the shelf. It was all coated with undisturbed dust. The room hadn't been cleaned properly for a long time. Old Arthur must have been running a skeleton staff, from what he had seen so far. Dust and cobwebs everywhere, an unkempt garden, bits falling off the roof. It all reinforced his conviction that the place was too expensive to run.

He turned back to the others and spotted yet another anomaly.

"Look at the tea tray! Jamset, you placed it down on that coffee table, and now it's on the sideboard."

"I don't think I did, sir. Are you sure you're alright? Should I fetch you a glass of brandy?"

"I thought you said you didn't have any brandy!" said Ronnie. "Do you or don't you? Because I'll have you know, I'm flat out."

He produced his hip flask, unscrewed the lid, turned it upside down and shook it to emphasise his plight.

"I was asking Mr Bradshaw, sir."

"Oh don't bother with him, he's sworn off it in a futile attempt to win back his woman. I, however, am footloose and fancy-free. Which means I can do as I like."

"Well, I'll need to get it from the cellar. The previous occupant was fiercely abstemious."

"Aah, the cellar! Yes, I've been looking forward to acquainting myself with that. You could call it the highlight of our visit, here. Tell you what, Jamset, save your legs, I'll go and find it myself. I am in serious need of libation."

"I hardly think that's appropriate, sir."

"I won't hear of it, you've done more than enough for us already. Take the rest of the evening off. Bernard shall accompany me. It will do him good to get away from the strange goings-on his overactive mind keeps imagining in this room."

"I'm not imagining anything. You would have seen these things yourself if you weren't so drunk. There are spirits in this room, I can sense them."

"I too can feel the calling of the spirits, my boy. Mine are, of course, of a different kind."

"Jamset told us to stay here," said Bernard.

"I did, sir," said Jamset. "It is a large house. You would not want to get lost."

"Ha, there's no danger of that," said Ronnie. "I am familiar with the layout of these places. I have mixed with the highest in the land."

"Really, sir?" said Jamset sceptically.

"Yeah," said Bernard. "He once went on a day trip to Longleat Safari Park and saw the Marquess of Bath through the car window."

"A poor gag, Bernard. You'll need to come up with better than that if you insist on pursuing this comedic career. Now, tell me. Are you going to follow the orders of a mere servant and sit around bored in here or come with me and take a gander around your new home?"

"I suppose a little wander couldn't do any harm."

"That's my boy. I suggest we start with the cellar. Now let us get down there before the judgemental spirits of temperance begin to coalesce."

With that, Ronnie strode with purpose towards the drawing-room door, with Bernard following reluctantly behind. Just before he reached the door, he turned back to speak to Jamset again.

"Just one thing, Jamset. Where is the cellar?"

"I thought you said you knew your way around these places?" said Bernard.

"The cellar is down the hall and on the left, sir," said Jamset. "The red door."

"Marvellous. Come, Bernard, let us explore your ancestral pile."

Leaving Jamset behind, they followed his directions until they found the cellar door, just before the entrance to the kitchens to the rear of the house. It opened to reveal a stone staircase, leading downwards. The steps were made of crudely hacked rock, and were steep and uneven.

It didn't help that there didn't appear to be any light source, so they were reliant on what was filtering down from the hallway above. Ronnie led the way, but it was a long way down and the deeper they went, the darker it got.

Just as Bernard was thinking of suggesting that they went back and asked Jamset to put the lights on, they reached the bottom. He began fumbling around on the wall, for a light switch, but to no avail.

"Bloody hell, it's dark down here," he remarked.

"Nonsense," replied Ronnie. "You could have done with a few years in the army like me. They trained us to see in the dark."

Ronnie promptly tripped over some unseen furniture and went down like a sack of spuds.

"Didn't train you very well, did they?" said Bernard, laughing at Ronnie's predicament, as he flailed around on the floor. It felt like the first time he had laughed in months. Perhaps Ronnie was right. Maybe this trip was what he needed. His co-star might have been an obnoxious and embarrassing individual, but he did possess a certain comedic value.

"Shut up and help me up," said Ronnie, who wasn't seeing the funny side.

Bernard made his way over to the desk that Ronnie had tripped over, where he spotted something in the dim light that might shed some light on their situation.

"Hey, I think I've found a torch."

"For God's sake turn it on then. I think I've done myself a bloody rupture."

Bernard fiddled with the torch, trying to find the mechanism, eventually shining a light onto the prone Ronnie. After helping him up, he shone it around to try to get a feel for their surroundings.

"That's better," said Bernard. "I'll have a look around and see if I can find a light switch. There must be one down here somewhere."

He scanned the walls with the torch but didn't find what he was looking for. Hadn't Arthur made any effort to modernise the house? He tried the other side of the cellar, and that was when the torch illuminated racks and racks of wine, stretching out in front of them.

"Bloody hell, I should have left it off," he said, knowing what the inevitable response from Ronnie would be.

"Good Lord!" exclaimed Ronnie. "Look at all that wine!! Perhaps I died in the fall and I've gone to heaven!"

"It's heaven for you perhaps, but hell for me. I can't drink any of it."

The discovery of the wine led to Ronnie making a miraculous recovery. All signs of any supposed injury sustained in his recent fall vanished in a flash as he couldn't get to the wine racks fast enough. He pulled a bottle from the rack at random and perused the label.

"Bernard, I do wish you would cease your endless carping. Just because you've decided you don't want to drink anymore doesn't give you the right to spoil everyone else's fun. Now bring that torch over here, I want to take a closer look at this stuff.

Bernard did as he asked, bringing the torch closer so that Ronnie could read the labels. He took out his pince-nez and picked up two or three bottles in turn. What he saw was extremely agreeable.

"Look at this stuff, Château Lafite Rothschild, Leoville-Las Cases, Veuve Clicquot. Tremendous! Old Arthur may not have drunk, but he knew his wines."

Bernard tried not to think about the wine. Staying off the booze was bad enough under normal circumstances, and being almost surrounded by it didn't help, especially when it was vintage high-quality stuff. Then he noticed something on the wall behind the wine racks.

"I couldn't see a light switch anywhere," he said. "But look over there on the walls. Old-fashioned candelabras. Here, pass me some matches."

There were three candelabras, spaced at regular intervals, each holding two candles. He walked over to them, pulled out a box of matches and lit each one in turn. Then he turned back to Ronnie, who was still poring over the wines.

"That's better, I can see them properly now. My goodness, this is absolutely extraordinary. Come and look at this bottle of Château Lafite."

"I'm not too knowledgeable on wine, Ronnie."

"You wouldn't be, boy. It's a class thing. Allow me to enlighten you. Look at the date on the bottle. It's an 1869 vintage! This is practically the holy grail of wine."

"Is it valuable, then?"

"Priceless, my boy, priceless. We have struck gold. If it's real, that is."

"What do you mean, if it's real?"

"Look at the bottle. It looks brand new. How can it be? This bottle of wine is over a hundred years old. There is not a speck of dust or a cobweb in sight which is surprising when you consider the state of the rest of the house. I think the first thing you need to get when you move in here is a decent cleaning lady."

"Who said anything about moving in here?" said Bernard. "I live and work in Manchester, remember?"

Ronnie began to examine some of the other bottles.

"They've all got similar dates and they all look brand new. How odd."

"I am sure there is some logical explanation," said Bernard. "Maybe Jamset comes down here and dusts them regularly.

"Shame he doesn't do the same with the rest of the house but never mind. There are more important considerations, for example, what do they taste like? Let's get this Château Lafite uncorked."

"Are you mad? You can't open that. You said yourself, it's priceless."

"There are hundreds of bottles in here. Thousands, even. You aren't going to miss one. Now give me the corkscrew."

"What corkscrew?"

"Rule number thirty-five, Bernard. Never go anywhere without a corkscrew."

"You'll have one with you, then. Unless you've broken your own rule."

"I left it in Pat Phoenix's dressing room after a rather lively after-show party a couple of weekends ago."

"Looks like you'll have to go thirsty, then."

"Maybe not. Where's the brandy? Jamset said there was some down here. I'll have to see if I can find some."

Bernard wandered over to examine an extremely sophisticated-looking typewriter on a desk over by the far wall. It had a screen built into it and contained a lot of additional keys with mysterious labels such as F5 and Esc. The brand, ACER, was also unfamiliar to him.

There were a couple more candles in holders on the desk so he took the opportunity to light them too.

"This typewriter looks brand new too. I've never seen one like this before. It looks like something out of *Star Trek*."

"I wouldn't know, I've never watched it. It probably belongs to the manscrvant. They have all kinds of new-fangled gadgets out in the Far East."

"If you had been listening, you would know that Jamset is born and bred in Britain, so that scuppers that theory."

"Look, someone's left a half-drunk mug of coffee next to it," said Ronnie, touching the white mug he had spotted next to the futuristic typewriter.

"That's interesting," he said. "It's still warm."

"Perhaps you should drink it. It might help you sober up."

Dismissing the suggestion, Ronnie turned and walked back to the wine racks, to see if he could find any brandy among the bottles. With his back now turned, the ghost of a Civil War Cavalier, carrying a musket, appeared in the middle of the room directly in front of Bernard. Quickly, it seemed to stride across the cellar and towards the wall, close to the stairway via which they had entered the cellar.

"Look, Ronnie, look!" he cried.

"Now what is it?" said Ronnie, turning around. But once again, he was too late to spot what Bernard had seen. The ghostly figure had disappeared straight through the wall as if it wasn't there.

"A ghost! A ghost! A bloody Cavalier! Like from the Civil War! He had the floppy hat and long curly hair and everything."

"Here we go again. There's nothing there."

"He was right there. He just walked through the wall over there."

Bernard walked over to the point where the Cavalier had disappeared and put his hands up against the wall, but it was just solid rock. The image he had seen hadn't been solid, though. It had been semi-transparent as if it was only half there. That was why he had naturally referred to it as a ghost. It had appeared exactly as he had seen them portrayed in films.

Ronnie merely shook his head in disbelief and turned his attention back to the wine where he was pulling the bottles out one by one.

"There's no bloody brandy. Jamset has been taking the piss. Isn't there anything here without a cork?"

"They don't make wine with screw caps," said Bernard.

"Well, they bloody ought to. It can't be that difficult. If they can do it with whisky, surely they can do it with wine."

"I think some of the cheap stuff has screw caps."

"I don't drink the cheap stuff. And there's not going to be any down here. It's bloody ridiculous. All this wine and no way of opening it."

"Water, water, everywhere, and not a drop to drink, eh?"

"An erroneous choice of quotation, Bernard. Don't try to be poetic, it doesn't suit you. Stick with the limericks, they are more appropriate for your fan base. Now how am I going to get this bloody wine open?"

"I think we've got more important things to worry about, don't you?"

"Like your delusions? I'm sorry but it's time you were put straight. You are hallucinating. You have been all day. I can only conclude it's a combination of alcohol withdrawal, your bleeding heart, and those happy pills you've been taking. They've affected your mind. All these apparitions are just fig leaves of the imagination. You need to snap out of it and be more like me. Fearless and bold."

"Foolhardy would be a more accurate description," replied Bernard.

Ronnie had pulled out half the bottles in the rack by now, but the latest one he had grabbed hold off was stubborn. It was almost as if it was attached to the wall.

"This bottle's stuck Come on, ya bugger! Come to Daddy!"

He gave it an almighty pull and then there was an ominous rumbling sound. Across the cellar, the wall where the Cavalier had disappeared swung open to reveal a secret passage.

"Look at that," said Bernard. "What did I tell you? This place is bloody haunted, mate."

"Tish and pish. It will be an old priest's hole. They're common in houses from this period."

"Well, I want to have a look. Whatever is down there, someone wanted it concealed. Why else would you hide the mechanism to open it in the wine rack? It could be a secret passage to somewhere, or there could be some hidden treasure."

"Admittedly, that would be an agreeable outcome," conceded Ronnie.

"It's better than staying in here. All these bloody spirits and spectres are freaking me out."

"Freaking you out? Where do you get these frightful expressions from? I suspect you have been watching too much transatlantic television. May I also point out the flaw in your plan? You claim your ghostly Cavalier went through the wall right where that passage is. Far from getting away from him, won't this lead you back towards him? Assuming he exists of course. Which he doesn't."

"Look, there's a secret passage right there in front of us waiting to be explored. Who wouldn't want to investigate? If you don't want to, you can stay here. I'm not bothered, either way."

"In the absence of a corkscrew, there's not much point in me staying here, is there? You can go in front, though. It's pitch dark in there."

"What happened to you being fearless and bold?"

"I am, but you're the one with the torch, idiot."

"Oh yeah."

"Come on then, let's have at it. And just in case the batteries die, I think we should take one of these."

Ronnie grabbed one of the candle holders from the desk and they began to make their way along the narrow tunnel. It sloped downhill and twisted and turned at sharp angles in places. Bernard wondered how far it would stretch. It was most certainly more than just a priest's hole. Then, they took a tight turn to the right, and Bernard could see they were almost at the end.

"Hey, look, there's a light up ahead," he said, shining the torch on a bright arch-shaped opening ahead of them.

"Good, hopefully we'll pop up in the pub. In the cellar, ideally, then I can refill my flask."

"We haven't gone anywhere near far enough to be under the pub. I mean, honestly, do you ever stop thinking about booze?"

"No. Except when I'm thinking about women. But booze usually comes first in the pecking order."

They emerged through the archway at the end of the passage into a pentagonal chamber, with five exits, each being an arch identical to the one through which they had just come. The room was lit by flaming torches attached to the stone walls in between each archway. The rest of the room was empty, save for a large slab in the centre of the room. There was a single item on top of the slab; an amulet containing a red stone which seemed to be glowing slightly under its own luminescence.

"Wow, what on earth?" asked Bernard. "It looks like something out of *Doctor Who*."

"I'll have to take your word for that. You know you should get out more. I mean, watching children's television on a Saturday evening after opening time. Shocking."

"*Doctor Who* is not a children's programme. It's a family show."

"If you say so. Did you know they had me lined up for the gig after Patrick Troughton left? Sadly, they couldn't afford my fee so they gave it to Pertwee instead."

"Thank goodness for that," replied Bernard. "You'd have ruined it."

"I would have brought an air of much needed gravitas to the role."

"You would certainly have brought an air of something to the role. Anyway, forget all that. What do you think this place is?"

"Search me, old chum."

"Do you know what I think? Look around the room. Five arches and five huge stones between them. Do you remember what Brenda said about the missing stone circle? Perhaps we've just found it."

Curious, Bernard reached over to the slab and picked up the amulet. As soon as he touched it, the hooded figure he had first seen on the drive down and latterly in the graveyard emerged from one of the arches. But this time, it wasn't Bernard who saw it. Finally, one of the apparitions had appeared right in front of Ronnie who stared in stunned terror at the apparition, gibbering with fear.

"B-B-B-Bernard!"

"What's up?" asked Bernard, who couldn't take his eyes off the amulet. It was having a strange hypnotic effect on him.

"G-G-G-Ghost!" stuttered Ronnie.

"What? You've been watching too much *Scooby Doo*, mate!"

He tore his gaze away from the amulet to see Ronnie rooted to the spot, as the hooded figure extended a bony finger towards him. It looked just as it had when Bernard had first seen it, but unlike Ronnie, he didn't feel particularly afraid.

"A-ha! Told you! But you wouldn't believe me."

"We've got to get out of here!" shouted the terrified Ronnie. "Come on, Bernard, run!"

He screamed as the hooded figure began moving towards him, and ran off through one of the five arches.

Chapter Five
June 2022

Unlike Ronnie, Bernard felt strangely calm despite the seemingly perilous nature of the situation. He was fascinated by all the strange things he had seen. He also figured that if the hooded figure had been intending to kill him, it would have done so by now. This was the third time he had seen it, after all.

He was right, because as soon as Ronnie had left the scene, the apparition dissolved into nothingness, leaving no trace it had ever been there. But, by now, the panicked Ronnie was out of sight. Bernard called after him to return, but it was to no avail.

"Where are you going? It's gone now! Come back!

There was no sign of him coming back, so Bernard reluctantly followed him through the arch.

Consumed by fear, Ronnie ran back up the tunnel in the darkness. He stumbled on a couple of occasions and almost fell over again, but managed to make it back up to the cellar in one piece. It too was in darkness as the candles they had lit earlier were no longer burning. He didn't have his candle anymore either. He had dropped it when he had run from the chamber.

As slowly as he dared, he felt his way across the cellar and back to the staircase. As he neared the top, a light shone from behind him onto the cellar door. It was Bernard who was still carrying the battery power torch he had found earlier and had used it to light his way back to the cellar.

"Stop! It's gone now!" called Bernard. "Why are you running away? So much for your military training that you're always banging on about!"

But Ronnie ignored him. He had one thought, and one thought only – to get out of the house and back to the safety of his car.

He emerged into the hallway, passing Jamset, who had changed his outfit since he had last seen him. He was now dressed in a smart business suit rather than the traditional clothing of his ancestors which he had been wearing earlier. In his single-minded pursuit of sanctuary, though, this detail was irrelevant to Ronnie. Had he taken a moment to look around him he would have noticed many other changes too – a complete change in décor, for one, but he had eyes only for the front door.

Outside, he was horrified to discover that his car was nowhere to be seen. Had someone stolen it? Or perhaps Jamset had moved it to prevent him from escaping. He had been suspicious of the manservant from the start. Where exactly did he fit into all of this?

There was another car outside, but it was a type with which Ronnie was unfamiliar. It looked a bit like a Mini, but it was larger and of a different design. It was also painted in a gleaming red shade that looked almost metallic.

He paused for a moment in a rather befuddled state of mind. The layout of the garden in front of the house wasn't as he remembered it. The driveway seemed to have moved and he could have sworn there were some fountains out here before. Now it was all lawn and bushes. There was also a new gate, much closer to the house and it was closed, unlike the open entrance that had greeted them on first arriving. For all he knew, it could be locked.

How was he going to get out of here? He felt the sense of panic returning in his desperation to get away. Then he spotted a gap in the trees on the other side of the gardens, which might provide some temporary sanctuary. Anything to get away from the house and that awful skeletal thing.

It was evening, still some time until sunset, but it was overcast and getting quite gloomy outside. Once he reached the path that led into the woods it began to get dark very quickly. The woods were very overgrown and the natural canopy of the trees made it seem darker than it was. Although it wasn't yet night he could already hear owls hooting. Even more spookily, he could hear an unidentified animal howling somewhere deeper in the woods.

If anything, this was even more terrifying than the house. What sort of creatures lived out here? After what he had seen earlier, nothing was off the table now. The howling he had heard a moment ago could be a werewolf for all he knew, and with the noise he was generating as he crashed through the woods he could very well be attracting its attention. Then, just to top it all, it began to rain.

The path was getting rougher, with many brambles across it that threatened to tear his expensive clothes. In some places the path forked and he was forced to make a split-second choice as to which way to go. One wrong move and he might hit a dead end. Then he would be cornered prey for whatever that damned beast was that was still howling away. Sure enough, he twice had to retrace his steps after coming across fallen trees blocking the path.

At times it felt as if he was being channelled to go in a certain direction, like a rat in a maze. When the rain got heavier, and there was a flash of lightning followed by a dramatic clap of thunder, he felt like a doomed character in a cheesy horror film just waiting for the inevitable to happen. Only a couple of nights ago he had scoffed at one of these films on the television. It didn't seem very funny now.

He wished Bernard were with him. Much as he maligned his younger co-star, he needed him more than he would ever allow himself to admit. If Bernard was alongside him, he would know what to do and could get them out of the situation. Of course, Ronnie wouldn't lose face by giving him any credit for the rescue. That wasn't the way things worked between them. To acknowledge any sort of inferiority as to his standing in the relationship simply wasn't on.

Just as he was beginning to think he would be lost in the woods forever he saw the chink of the setting sun through the trees. The rain stopped almost instantly, and the path he was following emerged into the outskirts of the village. He had never been so relieved in all his life. He stopped for a moment, his heart going like the clappers and tried to regain his composure. Everything seemed normal. Bizarrely, there was barely a cloud in the sky and the ground was bone dry. Five minutes ago he had been in the middle of a thunderstorm but it looked as if it hadn't rained here today at all.

He walked towards the green and sat down on a bench. There was no sign of the earlier festivities. Perhaps they were all over. He put his head in his hands and tried to pull himself together. Then he heard a voice he had never been so happy to hear in all his life.

"Bloody hell, Ronnie. You nearly killed me. I've never seen you move so fast."

He looked up to see the reassuring figure of Bernard standing over him. He was sweating profusely, red in the face and there were beads of sweat forming on his forehead. Ronnie wasn't feeling too clever either. Neither man was remotely fit. Years of drinking, smoking and the late nights of an actor's life had seen to that.

Ronnie's remarkable burst of speed in his haste to depart the house had been driven predominantly by fear-induced adrenalin. Back in the safety of the village, he realised how out of breath he was. It was true, he hadn't moved like that in years. It was amazing what you could do when the chips were truly down. And they had been down, he was sure of that. He couldn't deny the evidence of his own eyes.

"I saw the hooded figure. It was hideous."

"Now you know what I've been on about all day," replied Bernard. "You see, I wasn't crazy after all, despite you trying to convince me that I was."

If Bernard was expecting an apology or even some sort of acknowledgement that he had been right, he was to be disappointed. That wasn't the Rathbone way, and now Ronnie had regained his composure there was only one thought on his mind.

"Well, after all the excitement, not to mention the exercise, I need a drink."

"You can drink back at the house. We need to be there at midnight and it's going to be dark soon. Come on. I'll even let you drink one of my vintage bottles if it makes you happy."

"Are you mad? I need the congeniality of an English pub, not your house of horrors."

"Go on then. Just a quick one," said Bernard, deciding to indulge him, just this once. He had just had a bit of a shock, after all. Perhaps a brandy or two might make him better disposed towards the idea of a return to the house.

"You know me."

They began to walk across the green toward the pub. One of the things about chocolate box villages like Weirdwell was that they changed very little over time. The basic structure around the village green was very much as it had appeared on their previous visit. However, had they been paying attention, they might have noticed a few things that were not as they should have been.

The cars were strange and futuristic, painted in bright colours with smooth, rounded designs. They were very different from the boxy British Leyland designs in the drab, matt colours they were used to seeing trundling up and down the Manchester streets.

Some of the cottages had strange black dishes attached to them, and their squat, metal dustbins had been replaced by ugly green plastic versions. The red phone box was still there but contained no telephone. Instead, it housed a collcction of old books.

But, full of thoughts of what had happened at the house, Ronnie and Bernard noticed none of this. All of that was to change as soon as they entered the pub which was barely recognisable from the place they had visited at lunchtime. Other than the wooden beams that lined the ceiling, the interior had been completely transformed.

"They've smartened this place up a bit since this afternoon," remarked Ronnie. "They must have refurbished it for the festival."

Bernard looked around, before replying.

"They can't possibly have done all that in one afternoon. The interior has been completely redesigned. Even the bar isn't in the same place."

"Perhaps we're in the wrong room," suggested Ronnie. "I do hope we haven't wandered into the saloon by mistake. That wouldn't do my reputation any good at all. You know I always drink in the lounge."

"I'm pretty sure there is only one bar in here."

"Look, they've had a bit of tidy up during the afternoon, that's all. It's not that different. I think the fear from what happened in that chamber has scrambled your memories, dear boy. Come on, let's get a drink."

"As I recall, you were the one that ran off screaming."

"Oh, that was just me practising for an audition. They are talking about doing a Hammer Horror stage show on Broadway next year and my agent reckons he can get me a part in it. Now come on, let's get those drinks. My throat is as dry as a nun's chuff."

"It hasn't taken you long to get back to normal, has it?"

"Would you expect any less?" asked Ronnie, very much back to his old self.

They walked up to the bar, but there was no sign of Brenda or Alan. Instead, there was a young man with a shaven head, a tight T-shirt, and tattoos all up his bare arms behind the bar. He was deep in conversation with a girl perched upon a barstool, who was as tattooed as he was.

When Ronnie caught sight of them, he recoiled in surprise at the man's appearance. In addition to the tattoos, he was covered with face piercings and had a long, pointy ginger beard. This wasn't the sort of person that Ronnie expected to find behind the bar of a country pub. Unless it was something to do with the festival. Yes, that would be it.

"My goodness, this chap's done a splendid job with the fancy dress for the festivities. Well done, sir. What are you? A pirate? And is this your wench?"

The tattooed man reacted in a manner that Ronnie had not been expecting.

"Are you taking the piss, grandad?"

"I beg your pardon? I am nobody's grandfather, at least not that I am aware of. Now if you could see your way to providing me with a large brandy, I shall overlook your slur on this occasion."

"Whatever you say, gramps," replied the barman as he turned to get the brandy. Ronnie wasn't impressed by the fellow's manners and he was also irked at being sworn at. That wasn't the level of customer service he demanded; however, the most important thing now was he got his hands on the drink. Until then, he would make light of the situation.

"That carnival makeup is jolly arresting, eh?" he said to Bernard. "Look at the fake tattoos on her! What's she meant to be, some sort of sailor girl or something?"

"I don't think it's makeup, Ronnie," said Bernard. "Those tattoos look real to me."

"On a woman? Ridiculous."

"It's not that unusual, Ronnie."

"On the types of women that you associate with, no doubt."

Bernard was having a good look around, confirming his suspicion that something was very wrong. There was nothing amiss with his memory. This was not the same place they had been this afternoon. Well, it was, but it wasn't. It was all very peculiar. Meanwhile, the barman had finished pouring Ronnie's drink and placed it on the bar in front of him.

"That'll be six quid please, old man."

"Six pounds? Have you taken leave of your senses, man? I asked for a glass, not a whole vat."

"I'm sure he's just kidding about the six pounds, Ronnie," said Bernard. "He probably meant six shillings. Everyone's got muddled up since this decimalisation business. Here you go."

Bernard reached into his pocket and produced a pound note, handing it over to the barman in the hope that this would resolve the situation. But instead it made it worse.

"What the fuck's that?"

Even Bernard was taken aback by the man's foul language. There was no need for it, even if Ronnie had wound him up, which was a frequent occurrence wherever they went. Even so, they rarely encountered this level of aggression.

"It's a pound note, mate. What do you think it is?"

"There's no such thing as a pound note. Now stop pissing me about and pay up – or fuck off."

Ronnie was about to release what he considered to be a devastating riposte when they were interrupted by another customer who had overheard the exchange and decided to intervene. He was a small man in late middle age, wearing round John Lennon-style glasses beneath a head of thinning, grey hair.

"Excuse me," said the man, timidly. "But it is you, isn't it? The legendary Ronald Rathbone?"

Ronnie's altercation with the barman was put on temporary hold as he looked this new arrival up and down. Although he generally considered fans a nuisance, if one wanted to flatter him with words such as legendary, he was happy to indulge them. And most importantly, there might be a drink in it.

"Ahh, at last, a man of breeding and discernment. Yes, it is I."

"Brilliant, I can't believe it, and you don't look any different."

"Different from what?"

"And Bernard! Bernard Bradshaw. Ey up!"

"Ey up!" replied Bernard, much to Ronnie's annoyance.

"Good God!" he exclaimed. If he never heard that catchphrase again it would be too soon. Just once it would be nice to upstage Bernard, but the new arrival seemed more interested in him now.

In the meantime, there was still the impatient, aggressive barman to deal with, who wasn't impressed by this display of fawning by one of his regulars over the two strangers.

"Oi! I'm still waiting. Are you going to pay for these drinks or not?"

"It's alright, Owen," said their excitable fan. "I'll get these."

"You'll need to re-mortgage your house to get a round in here, mate," said Bernard.

"Ah, well we need to support our country pubs, don't we? Use them or lose them, as they say. What'll it be? I'm Brian, by the way."

"Nothing for me thank you, Brian," said Bernard. "I don't drink."

"If you don't buy a drink, you can piss off," said Owen the barman. "This is a business, not a charity shop."

"Charming fellow," remarked Ronnie, looking around at the pub that had only about half a dozen customers in, including themselves. "No wonder business is booming."

"You could have a Diet Coke," suggested Brian.

"What an odd thing to say," said Bernard. "I'll have a Coke but I'm not on a diet."

"This is very kind of you, good sir," said Ronnie, buttering up his latest benefactor. "I shall join you in a large brandy. One which our friend here has already poured."

Ronnie put particular emphasis on the word friend to express his distaste for Owen. Then he watched, fascinated, as Brian waved his watch over a scanner which the barman was holding out in front of him. There was an audible beep, and seemingly that was it, with no cash changing hands. Bernard was watching too and took the opportunity to quiz Brian about it.

"What happened there? When your watch beeped?"

"I was paying for the drinks."

"With your watch?" asked Ronnie. "Where is your money?"

"What, you mean you've never seen an Apple Watch before?" asked Brian, with a tone of surprise that suggested it was an everyday occurrence.

"What's an Apple Watch?" asked Ronnie. "It sounds like some sort of game-keeping activity. Keeping the pesky kids out of the orchard, that sort of thing."

"Coke you can diet on and magic watches named after a fruit. What is going on here?" asked Bernard, who was beginning to get an inkling of what might have happened, but needed Brian to confirm it.

"Ah, very good," said Brian. "I get it. You're in character pretending you're from the 1970s. Are they making a documentary on *Sladen Square*? A sort of fifty-years-later kind of thing? I loved the show as a kid. I used to watch it with my nan. I must say you're both looking well. It's as if you haven't aged a day."

"Good clean living, man, that's the answer," said Ronnie. "Forty Stuyvesants a day, a bottle of brandy and the love of as many good women as you can lay your hands on. Or even better, bad ones."

Bernard's suspicions had been correct. He was in no doubt now as to what had happened. It was the stuff of science fiction, but then fact and fiction had been blurring all day, ever since he had first seen the hooded figure in the road.

"You said fifty years later," he said. "What exactly did you mean? What year do you think this is?"

"2022 of course. What other year could it be?"

This was all the confirmation Bernard needed, but Ronnie wasn't convinced.

"You jest, my friend! 2022 indeed. If it was, we'd all be living on the moon. I think you've had too much to drink."

He went to light up a Stuyvesant, to the fury of Owen behind the bar. He grabbed the soft drink dispensing hose and sprayed soda squarely in Ronnie's face, just as he was lifting the match to his mouth. Ronnie spluttered in surprise, dropping the now soggy cigarette, and glaring from his drenched face. For the second time today, the front of his tweeds had been soaked.

"Are you out of your tiny bloody mind, you foul-mouthed hooligan? What do you think you are doing?"

Owen pointed at a large sign above the bar which stated 'NO SMOKING' in large red letters.

"You are beginning to seriously get on my tits now, boomer," said Owen with a murderous look in his eye. "You know damn well you aren't allowed to smoke in here."

Things were threatening to turn distinctly nasty, but thankfully, once again, Brian came to their rescue.

"That's OK, Owen, I'll deal with it. Come on outside, Ronnie. You can smoke out there."

"Fine," replied Owen. "But I don't care for your choice of friends. One more step out of line and they are banned. And so are you."

Ronnie was seething as Brian hastily ushered him and Bernard outside.

"Here we go, Ronnie, you can puff away to your heart's content out here," said their new friend.

"A pub that bans smoking. I've never heard anything so ludicrous. It will never catch on," declared Ronnie confidently, pulling out another cigarette and lighting up.

"We are in 2022, then?" asked Bernard. "When exactly?"

"June 2022," replied Brian. "Midsummer's day to be precise. We used to have a huge festival every year on this date but the youngsters aren't that bothered about that sort of thing these days."

"I'm not surprised if they are anything like that thug in there," said Ronnie. "But look, you can't seriously expect us to believe that we're in 2022 just because you've bought me a brandy, which I hope will be the first of many."

"I think he's right," said Bernard. "I mean, six quid for a brandy? No smoking in pubs? Look around you. We may be in a little rural village, but the world is very different from how it was in 1972."

"All of that could have been faked. This could be an elaborate scheme to dupe me out of my money. Let me make it clear, that is not going to happen. Rule number sixty-three. No one cons Ronnie Rathbone."

"What about that bloke who sold you shares in that hotel in Torremolinos? You know, the one that didn't exist?"

"Quiet, Bernard. Now look here, Brian, I want to know what your game is. If you insist on sticking to this story that we have somehow ended up in the year 2022, I want to see some evidence."

"That's perfectly understandable," said Brian. "I would be sceptical in your position too. Maybe this will convince you. Have a look at this. Did you have anything like this in 1972?"

Brian pulled out a device from his pocket that was commonplace in 2022 but unfamiliar and futuristic to the eyes of Bernard and Ronnie. It was the latest iPhone, sleek and black. He unlocked it with a thumbprint and showed them the date on the front screen.

"I say, that's a rather clever calendar," said Bernard.

"Oh, it's far more than that. This is my smartphone."

"You keep a phone in your pocket?" asked Bernard.

"Everyone has one."

"You mean you can make phone calls on that thing? Without any wires?" Bernard was intrigued, as was Ronnie who leaned in for a close look.

"Yes, but I use it for messaging, mostly. And the internet. It's got 5G on it."

Bernard was doing his best to understand, using the language of fifty years ago, but technology had moved on to such an extent he was struggling to equate the terms Brian was using with the world he had come from.

"That's like, something to do with gravity, right?"

Brian paused, wondering how he could put it into terms that someone from 1972 would understand.

"No, 5G is like, well, think of it like invisible telephone wires in the air that work like radio waves. That's how we access the internet."

"And what's the internet?" enquired Bernard, who was full of questions. "Is it like a portable intercom system?"

"It's nothing so mundane as that. Since the 1990s, it has revolutionised the world. On this phone, you can find out the answer to anything you want to know. Imagine the largest library in the world full of encyclopaedias covering absolutely everything. And that's not all. You can order shopping, food, and pay for things. It's like having the whole world in your pocket."

"That's amazing. The future sounds incredible," replied Bernard.

"I still can't get my head around the idea that you have come here from 1972," said Brian.

"Just look at us," replied Bernard. "How could we not look any older? I'd be like, well, over ninety by now. Do I look over ninety?"

"Well, I'm not saying anything, but you have let yourself go a little since this Diane business, dear boy," said Ronnie.

"I did wonder why you looked exactly like you did in the 1970s," replied Brian. "I can't believe it – you truly have travelled in time! This is so exciting!"

Even Ronnie, who had been holding out up to this point, couldn't deny the reality of the situation. Now that he was on board with what was happening, he was already scheming to turn it to his advantage.

"Leaving this temporal abnormality aside for now, you said you could find out the answer to anything with that thing?" he asked.

"Of course," said Brian. "What do you want to know?"

"I just want to test it out," continued Ronnie. "Which horse won the Cheltenham Gold Cup in 1970?"

Ronnie looked on as Brian typed Cheltenham Gold Cup 1970 into a small bar on the screen. Within a couple of seconds, a photograph of a horse jumping a steeplechase fence and some accompanying text appeared.

"Here we are," said Brian. "The horse was called L'Escargot. That's French for snail, isn't it? Odd name for a horse."

"Ridden by?" asked Ronnie.

"Tommy Carberry."

"Odds?"

"33/1."

"He's right, you know," said Ronnie. "I remember it well. Amazing!"

"He would remember. He hasn't picked a winner since," said Bernard.

"Wait, there's more," said Brian. "He won the Grand National too, according to this."

"Really?" said Ronnie. "I don't remember that."

"Yes, in 1975."

Ronnie's eyes lit up at this information. He had just been given a cast iron tip for a race that, from his perspective, hadn't happened yet. With information like this, he could wipe the smile off the Colonel's face once and for all.

"Now that is worth remembering. These little devices are remarkable. What else do you have in this future of yours? An army of sex robots, catering to your every desire?"

"Err, no, they haven't developed those properly yet. I think they may have a few rudimentary ones in Japan."

"Well, so long as they're rude. Speaking of which, I met a rather lovely young Japanese filly, a while back. It was after an episode of *Top of the Pops*. I was filming for the BBC at the time and Jimmy Savile invited me to the after-show party. It was a cracking night, I can tell you. All the stars were there, big names like Gary Glitter, you name them."

Ronnie looked up to see Brian staring at him with a horrified look on his face. He was used to seeing such reactions from people to some of his remarks. They were usually prudish types who didn't appreciate the Rathbone candour. But this came as something of a surprise. He hadn't said anything particularly controversial in that last sentence, had he?

"Whatever is the matter with you, man?" he asked.

"Jimmy Savile and Gary Glitter?" replied Brian. "You must know about them? They are two of the worse sex offenders in history. Look at this."

Brian began to pull up news stories on his phone about the vile crimes perpetrated by people who in Ronnie's world were respected stars and entertainers. He couldn't believe what he was seeing and quickly realised he needed to dissociate himself from them. He began to backtrack, rather unconvincingly.

"Oh, er, did I say Jimmy Savile? Of course, I didn't mean him. Never met the bloke. Found him a bit creepy. On the telly, I mean, because as we already established, I most certainly do not know him in real life. Now I come to think of it, it was Ed Stewart presenting the show that night. And it wasn't Gary Glitter, it was one of those other chaps. Marc Bolan. He's alright, isn't he?"

He looked hopefully at Brian, hoping he wasn't going to reveal that Marc Bolan had turned out to be a serial killer or something, but the reply put his mind at ease.

"Yeah, they're both fine. Or rather, they were. Both are sadly no longer with us."

"Good. I mean, not good that they are dead, good that they turned out to be good eggs. So to recap, it was Ed Stewart and Marc Bolan I was hanging out with. Not Jimmy Savile and Gary Glitter. I just got mixed up there for a moment. I was rather drunk at the time. The old memory can play tricks after a few drinks, you know."

"I'm surprised you can remember anything, the amount you drink," said Bernard.

Ronnie ignored Bernard's jibe and decided to press Brian for some more information. It was all very well knowing the winner of the Grand National in 1975 but assuming they got back to 1972, that would still be three years away. He needed something more immediate.

"Now then, let's get back to these horses. Let me see now, 1972. What big races are coming up? I know, can you look up who won the Northumberland Plate that year?"

Bernard had cottoned on to what Ronnie was up to and he didn't approve.

"Ronnie, can you leave your gambling addiction out of this for now? We must get back to the house. It'll be pitch dark soon."

"Hang on, hang on. Let me find this out first. It's all very well for you, with your inheritance, but you don't begrudge me making a little out of this jaunt, do you? After I've made the effort to come all this way?"

"Listen, I need to go for a slash," said Brian. "Why don't you look it up yourself? I'll leave you my phone while I pop to the Gents. Look up whatever you want."

"Get another round in on the way back," said Ronnie.

"Another round?" said Bernard. "Didn't you hear what I just said? We need to get going. I don't fancy trying to find my way back to the house in the dark."

"No rush, dear boy. Same again please, Brian, if that ignoramus behind the bar can manage it."

Brian headed back into the pub, which now had indoor toilets. The outside block that Bernard had used in 1972 had been demolished. Meanwhile, Ronnie was tapping away at the phone screen. The technology might have been new to him but it was remarkably easy to use. He just copied what he had seen Brian already do. All he had to do was type whatever he wanted to know into this Google thing and it would direct him to the information.

"Well, this might be a more worthwhile trip than I had anticipated," he remarked.

"Look, if we're going to be here a while then let's go inside and sit down. I'm still knackered after all that running and you can't smoke while you are busy with that thing."

"As you wish, dear boy, as you wish."

Ronnie led the way back inside, still glued to the phone, almost walking into the door frame as he went. This little machine was a goldmine. He couldn't understand why

Bernard hadn't cottoned on to the possibilities. Still, what could one expect from the working classes? They had no ambition, no inspiration. That's why they were the working classes. It was in the breeding.

Back in 1972, the Colonel was watching a news report on the television about the war in Vietnam. He had slipped into something more comfortable now, his smoking jacket, and was enjoying a large Cuban cigar. Then the phone rang again. He reached across and answered it in the usual manner.

"Hello, Berman's Dry Cleaning? Ah, Charles! What news?"

Charlie had left Ken watching the house and gone back into the village to use the phone box. By now the celebrations had become rather boisterous on the village green, thanks to the copious amounts of local ales and ciders that had been consumed. Some sort of ritual dance was now taking place around a large bonfire and it was hard to hear what his employer was saying over the hubbub in the background.

"They've gone inside some big posh stately home and they haven't come out. They've been in there for hours, Colonel."

"Really? A stately home? There's more to this than meets the eye. What is that fellow Rathbone up to? Keep them under surveillance and let me know if anything unusual occurs."

"Are you coming down here, chief?"

"No, I have pressing business to attend to here, keep me posted. Ciao for now."

The Colonel put down the phone and stubbed out the remainder of his cigar as a scantily clad Thai girl came through from the kitchen. She was carrying a tray containing two exotic-looking cocktails, decorated with umbrellas and skewers of mixed fruits.

"There you are, my dear," remarked the Colonel, patting the space on the sofa beside him. "Now, where were we again?"

At the pub, Ronnie and Bernard had settled in a rather cosy area of the pub full of soft furnishings and close to a disused fireplace. Bernard had slumped down in the middle of a sofa where he had begun rambling on about Diane again.

An uninterested Ronnie was far more interested in the phone but made appropriate soothing noises at regular intervals to try to pretend he was listening. He didn't want to engage with Bernard as that would detract him from the task at hand. He had done all the research he needed on the gambling front and was now exploring some of the other delights the machine in his hand had to offer.

Brian had returned from the toilets and was at the bar, while Bernard continued to ramble on.

"I realise now that it was my fault. I cocked it all up. It was all me. I pushed her away, and I disappeared for weeks on end, drinking myself daft. I abandoned her and when I came back up for air she'd moved on. I can't argue with anything that she's said. I told her I'd be happier on my own, and I got my wish. Thing is, I'm not happy. I don't think I'll ever be happy again"

"Porn! You can get porn on it!" exclaimed Ronnie excitedly. "I wouldn't need to make any more surreptitious trips to the Greek newsagents on Mill Street if I had one of these things."

"You haven't listened to a word I've said, have you?" said Bernard, irritated at the interruption.

"Look, Bernard. Some people need saving from themselves. Forget about Diane. Once we get back to 1972 I shall take you to one of my clubs and set you up with a nice chubby blonde or three. You'll soon feel better, I promise."

"No thank you, I know all about the sort of people that go to your dodgy clubs. Anyway, look at the clock. It's after ten and we need to go."

"Ah, splendid, here's Brian with the drinks," said Ronnie.

"Here we go, Ronnie," said Brian eagerly. "Another large brandy."

"Excellent," said Ronnie, snatching the glass off him rather rudely and draining it in one."

"Nice to meet you, Brian, but sorry, we've got to split," said Bernard, much to Ronnie's annoyance.

"Split?" exclaimed Ronnie. "Still you persist in utilising these vulgar terms! It is time for us to depart, my boy, to depart. Not to split!"

"Oh that's a shame," said Brian. "I was going to tell you about seeing Diane the other week."

"Diane?" replied Bernard, excitedly. "She's still alive, then? Maybe I could track her down here in 2022."

"Don't be ridiculous!" exclaimed Ronnie. "She'll be some wizened old crone by now. She had a distinct air of Mother Teresa about her back in 1972."

"Well, if we had time I would, but for now, as I have said several times, we need to get back to the house," said Bernard.

"Fair enough, time and tide wait for no man. 2022 has been a hoot, but I want to go back somewhere where I can get change from a pound note for a couple of drinks. And I have a little business to conduct in 1972, thanks to you, Brian."

"Speaking of which, haven't you forgotten something?" said Brian.

"Let me guess, you want an autograph?" suggested Ronnie. "It happens all the time."

"No. My phone, although we could all have a selfie together before you go."

"What a disgusting suggestion. Any selfies you wish to partake in I suggest you perform in the privacy of your boudoir. Here is your device. We're out of here."

"A selfie is a photograph that you take yourself," explained Brian. "Just a quick one?"

"Very well, if we must," said Ronnie.

They grouped around as Brian took the photo, although Ronnie refused to smile, putting on his serious actor face.

"Thanks," said Brian. "It was lovely to meet you both. Hope to see you again."

Ronnie and Bernard made their way towards the door. Just as they were leaving, they heard Owen call out behind them.

"Don't come again."

"Dreadful man," said Ronnie as soon as they were outside. "No customer service skills whatsoever. And as for that nauseating hanger-on, Brian, the further away we get from him, the better. I never could stand fans, loathsome creatures wanting bloody autographs all the time."

"You truly are an ungrateful sod," said Bernard. "You weren't complaining when he was buying you drinks."

"That was for his benefit. It makes these little people happy when they get the chance to reward their heroes. Now come along. We have an inheritance waiting for us."

"Us, don't you mean me?"

"Of course," said Ronnie. "A slip of the tongue."

"Yes, you have a lot of those."

Bernard looked across the green to where they had emerged from the woods earlier. It was fully dark now, and he couldn't say that the journey held much appeal. It had been bad enough before, and it had been still daylight then.

"Bloody hell, we've got to get back to the house on foot. We lost the car, remember? Either we go back through the woods or we risk life and limb on the main road in the dark."

"Let me stop you there, old chap. While you were wittering on about your love life I took the liberty of ordering an Uber on Brian's phone. A fiendish little device that. Shame he wanted it back."

"What's an Uber when it's at home?"

"This is," said Ronnie, as a car of a make Bernard had never heard of, a Kia, pulled up next to them.

"All very well, but how do we pay for it?" asked Bernard. "Our old coins and notes are out of date."

"Paid up front," said Ronnie. "Or rather, Brian did. He won't mind. He likes me."

"He's one of the few people who do," said Bernard as they got into the car, which swiftly pulled away, taking them back to the house.

Chapter Six
June 2022

The modern Kia took them swiftly back to the house, most of which was in darkness. The only light was coming from what by Bernard's estimation must be the drawing room.

"Surly fellow," remarked Ronnie, irked at their driver who had barely grunted a word of acknowledgement at Ronnie's attempts to start a conversation.

"I don't think he appreciated you addressing him as 'guvnor' in that cockney accent," replied Bernard.

It was a cloudy night in 2022, with no moon to light the way. Once the car had pulled away, the only illumination they had to go by was that which was flooding through the drawing-room window. It was enough for them to see the car outside that Ronnie had noticed earlier. He had been right to notice the similarity to the original Mini, but this was one of the larger, twenty-first-century editions.

"Still no sign of my bloody car, I see," said Ronnie. "Thieving bastards they are in the countryside. Don't be fooled by all that decent honest country folk patter they give you."

"Obviously, your car is not going to be here. We're in 2022, remember? Your car is probably still right where you left it, in 1972. You can't expect it to have been waiting here for fifty years for you to come back. And if it was, imagine what sort of state it would be in. A rusty hulk, full of weeds, no doubt. Now, let's get inside, get back to our own time and sort all this out."

After a couple of hours away from the house, the two of them had relaxed to some degree after their earlier ghostly encounters. However, now they had returned the strange apparitions were about to begin haunting them once again.

As Bernard led the way towards the front door, the shimmering image of a decrepit old man, with white hair and a matching beard, materialised in front of him. The ghost was holding his right hand up, palm outstretched, clearly trying to get him to stop. He could also see the man mouthing the words 'stay away,' but no sound was emanating from its lips.

Frustratingly, as on most of the previous occasions, Ronnie missed it. He had bent down to tie his shoelace just as the vision appeared. Despite Bernard becoming used to these supernatural events by now, he had still been slightly startled by the man's sudden appearance. He took a step backwards, knocking Ronnie over just as he was straightening back up.

"Now what are you playing at?"

Ronnie struggled to his feet, by which time the image of the old man had disappeared.

"It was another ghost," said Bernard. "He was right there in front of me. It wasn't one I'd seen before. He looked like some wise old seer. I think he was trying to warn us off going back in the house."

"Hmm, I'm still not convinced you're not imagining a lot of this. But, we don't have much choice, do we, not if we want to get home. Come on, let's go back inside. I'm getting thirsty. And I've come equipped this time."

He reached into his pocket and triumphantly produced a corkscrew.

"Where did you find that?"

"I liberated it from the pub when that tattooed yobbo wasn't looking. Now come on, let's go and sample that wine."

They made their way up to the front door to discover it ajar so Bernard tentatively pushed it open. He was a little unsure about entering unannounced. They had legitimate reasons for being there in 1972 but that had been fifty years ago. What would the current proprietors make of them entering uninvited?

And what about Jamset? Bernard remembered seeing him on the way out, albeit in different clothing but surely it couldn't have been the same Jamset. Perhaps it was a descendant, his son, or grandson maybe? It was just one of the mysteries about all of this that they were yet to get to the bottom of.

His first instinct was to go straight back down to the cellar and try to find their way back to their own time, but he couldn't help wondering about the lights on in the drawing room. He stopped in the centre of the hall weighing it up, as Ronnie strode past him in his enthusiasm to get back downstairs. Would it do any harm to go and speak to whoever was in the drawing room? There was the danger that they might be accused of trespassing. But on the upside, the people who lived here now might be able to shed some light on exactly what was going on. If they lived here, they must be aware of the strange nature of the house, mustn't they?

He made his decision and turned left, heading towards the drawing room, as Ronnie continued onwards. He wasn't afraid of the ghosts down there anymore, in fact, he had convinced himself that they didn't even exist. He had only seen the one and that could easily have been an alcohol-induced illusion. It wouldn't have been the first time.

As for Bernard's multiple claims of seeing spirits, he rationalised them as being down to the younger man's fragile emotional state. Yes, it was all nonsense but the wine was real and he was long overdue the chance to sample it. But just as he reached the cellar door, Bernard called him back.

"Hey! Ronnie! This way."

"Bloody hell," replied Ronnie, looking back to see Bernard disappearing up the corridor that led to the drawing room. Where was the fool going now? It seemed he was fated never to get his hands on that wine. He was tempted to ignore Bernard and go down to the cellar without him but decided against it. It wasn't that he was scared. After all the ghosts weren't real, he had already decided that, but it was best they stayed together.

"Wait for me," he called, striding rapidly back across the hallway to catch up with Bernard.

As Bernard had expected, there were indeed people in the drawing room. Two young women in their mid-twenties, had been exploring the room, similarly to the way that Ronnie and Bernard had when they first arrived, fifty years before. Very little, if anything, had changed in that time. The room was pretty much the same as they had left it, with no trappings of the modern world.

One of the women had strikingly bright blue and spiky hair. She sported a green T-shirt with the slogan 'Plant Based' displayed across it, and jeans with rips at regular intervals. She was standing in the centre of the room looking down at the floor beneath her with a look of horror on her face.

"OMG, look at this, Jocasta. I can't believe what I'm standing on."

She gestured at the tiger skin rug beneath her feet, as Jocasta, who sported dreads and wore a rainbow T-shirt with black canvas trousers, came over to examine it.

"What is it, Abigail? Oh, my! That's not real animal skin, is it? That's disgusting. I think I'm going to be sick."

An ornament on the mantelpiece had also caught Abigail's eye, and she wandered over to the mantelpiece to pick it up.

"And this is made from actual ivory. Your uncle was a sick man, Jocasta. You do realise you'll have to dispose of this stuff when you inherit the house, don't you? If you don't, you'll have blood on your hands."

She put the ornament down and wandered over to the bookshelf, which Bernard had examined before. She pulled out a book at random to examine it, further fuelling her outrage.

"And this is even worse! Just look at the title: *Eighteenth-Century British Colonialism*. That confirms it. This house was built on the profits of slavery. I can't allow you to inherit this. You'll be betraying generations who suffered at the hands of your wicked ancestors."

This was the moment when Ronnie and Bernard entered the room. The former's lascivious eyes were instantly drawn to the young women, despite what in his eyes was a questionable choice of clothing. He disapproved of Abigail's ripped jeans right away. She looked like some sort of ragamuffin. Still, looking on the bright side, if she was so poor she had to walk around in ripped clothes, then she might appreciate some attention from a man of his distinction. It was time to put the old Rathbone charm into action.

"Well, hello! And what do we have here?"

The two women turned around, surprised to see the new arrivals. They had been led to believe that there was only them and Jamset, the well-dressed butler who had greeted them, in the house.

"I'm Jocasta, and this is Abigail," said the dreadlocked girl, eyeing the new arrivals with suspicion. Neither woman was giving off particularly friendly vibes, but Ronnie seemed oblivious and continued regardless.

"Well, I must say, how wonderful it is to make the acquaintance of two such fine fillies, even if you are dressed somewhat inappropriately for a house of this stature. Now, I don't know if you're aware but there are some rather fine wines in the cellar here. Why don't we uncork a couple, relax, and get to know each other a little better?"

Bernard looked on with a familiar sense of foreboding that this wasn't going to end well.

"Fillies? How dare you be so sexist?" said Abigail, turning round to replace the book on the shelf, a move which gave Bernard a strange sense of déjà vu. Unfortunately, Ronnie was more interested in her posterior, and as always blurted out his reaction, oblivious to the likely reaction.

"Cor! Nice arse!"

"You vile and disgusting man!" exclaimed Abigail, angrily, turning back around. "How dare you! I've never felt so violated in all my life. Do you know, I've got a good mind to call the police. That's assault, that is."

"Assault? Nonsense, woman, I'm standing ten feet away. I haven't laid a finger on you. How can it be an assault?" He looked across to Bernard for moral support, giving a theatrical rolling of the eyes as he did, which was also picked up on by Abigail.

"There you go again!" she said. "That's a microaggression in itself. You'll go behind bars for this."

"Seriously? Has a man never paid you a compliment before? I was simply admiring your pert buttocks, where is the harm in that? Sid James does it all the time and the last time I looked he wasn't in prison. And as if the police would be interested, anyway. They've got more important things to do, like catching bank robbers, for example."

"Ronnie, give it a rest," said Bernard. "Now just shut up for a minute. I want to check something out."

He wandered over to the bookshelf to look at the book that Abigail had just replaced on the shelf. What he saw confirmed his suspicions. He turned back to the others to see Abigail and Jocasta looking daggers at Ronnie.

He signed, knowing that yet again he was going to have to try to smooth things out. Everywhere they went it was the same. He had come in here hoping to find some people to talk to who might know more about this strange house. These two were hardly likely to be much help now Ronnie had rubbed them up the wrong way. The way he talked to people was intolerable and he was tired of making excuses for him when there was no excuse.

He turned to Jocasta, who seemed the less aggressive of the two, and tried to appeal to her better nature.

"Please forgive my friend, he's a little old-fashioned. Do you mind if I ask what you're doing here?"

It was a lame attempt at an apology, but to his surprise she was willing to engage with him.

"I got a letter telling me to come to the house. It said that my Uncle Bernard had died and I was in line to inherit the estate."

"Bernard? But that's my name. And this is my estate. Or it soon will be."

"Well, you can't be the same Bernard. He was in his nineties. I mean, I never met him, so I don't know what he looked like, but you're far too young. The name must just be a coincidence."

Abigail was still furious at the things Ronnie had said and was not happy that Jocasta was talking to Bernard. Admittedly, Bernard might not have said or done anything she considered offensive but she assumed he was friends with the other monstrous man. In her eyes, that was more than sufficient to tar him with the same brush.

"Jocasta, please don't indulge these awful men. I don't think I can bear to be in the room with them any longer, particularly this one," she said, casting a disgusted look in Ronnie's direction.

"Oh do stop wittering on, woman," said Ronnie. "You know what you need, don't you? A damned good seeing to. A swift dose of the Rathbone should cure your hysteria."

Bernard dropped his head in despair. So much for smoothing things over.

"That's it! We refuse to stay here a moment longer," declared Abigail. "Come along, Jocasta."

Abigail stormed out of the room, with her friend trailing behind her. As Jocasta passed, Bernard noticed that she was wearing a necklace containing a jewel identical to the one they had found in the chamber. That interested him. Could there be some sort of connection? He wanted to ask her but decided it might be prudent to leave it under the current circumstances.

"That went well," he said despondently, as soon as Abigail and Jocasta had left the room.

"Pathetic," replied Ronnie. "The police indeed. Just for a little harmless flirting."

"That was not harmless flirting, Ronnie. You were offensive, sexist, and downright disgusting, even by your low standards. And remember, this is a different century, times may well have changed."

"It's a bloody awful century if you ask me. You can't smoke in the pub, you can't chat women up, and everyone dresses like bloody vagabonds. There was nothing wrong with anything I said just now, they just didn't appreciate my sense of humour."

"Ronnie, what you said wasn't acceptable in 1972, let alone now."

"Bollocks, all women love it. Especially when they hear it from the legendary Ronnie Rathbone. What woman wouldn't go weak at the knees, presented with this?"

He performed a flourishing hand gesture in front of his ample frame as Bernard looked on, marvelling at the extent of Ronnie's delusional sense of self-importance.

"I don't even know where to start with that. But please, don't ever embarrass me like that again. Now then, there are a couple of things I want to talk about. For a start, did you see her putting that book back on the shelf?"

"I was rather distracted by her lovely posterior at the time, old sport. Such a shame she didn't appreciate my compliments."

"You see, this is exactly the sort of thing I'm talking about. Can you please be serious and listen, just for one minute?"

"As you wish, dear boy. Do continue."

"When we first came in here, I saw a book floating through the air and placing itself on the shelf. I just checked and it was the very same book that Abigail was putting back in the same place, And what about this Uncle Bernard business? She said he was over ninety. I'm in my forties so it stands to reason. It must have been me."

"Well look on the bright side, at least you lived to a ripe old age. Perhaps the studio stumped up for a new liver because I can't envisage that one you've got in there lasting another half-century."

"I've told you, I'm off the sauce for good, Ronnie."

"That remains to be seen. I don't think you've got the same willpower to stay off it that we Rathbones possess."

"So says the man who has been swigging booze all day. If you had stayed sober you might have noticed something else. Look out the window."

"What for? To look at some grass and a few shrubs? It's hardly the Hanging Gardens of Babylon. Unless they've got some pampas grass out there. That could make things interesting."

"The point is that it's broad daylight outside. It was dark when the Uber dropped us off. And look at the clock. It's gone back to 7pm."

"It is a mystery, old chap, I'll give you that. Still, there's not much point hanging around here any longer is there? That little strumpet's not going to put out, so we may as well go back down to the cellar. At least we can have a drink down there."

"Are you sure you're not scared to go back down there? You ran away last time."

"A tactical withdrawal, Bernard, a tactical withdrawal. We know what to expect now, don't we? All we need to do is to go back to the chamber, through the correct door, and back into our own time. Then we simply wait it out until midnight, collect the loot, and all my, I mean your, worries will be over."

"That's interesting," said Bernard, who was still looking out of the window and had noticed a car coming along the driveway towards the house.

"It's that overgrown mini we saw earlier," said Ronnie. They watched as the car pulled up outside and Jocasta and Abigail got out.

"Do you think they went to the police?" asked Ronnie. "If so, there's no sign of them. I told you they wouldn't be interested."

"I don't think they've been anywhere near the police," replied Bernard. "I think they are only just arriving for the first time. What with time going back and everything."

"Right, if that's the case, surely they won't remember anything I said before. It will be as if they had never met us. The slate will be wiped clean and I can have another crack at them. I'll try a different strategy this time. Compliment them on their hair or something, that normally goes down well. Not that blue hair and dreadlocks are my thing, but they don't need to know that."

"Absolutely not, Ronnie. Those two and you are poles apart. You're from different centuries, to begin with, and even if you weren't, you are way too old for them. Never in a month of Sundays will either of them be interested in you. I think it would be better for all concerned if you were not to have any more interaction with them. Just chalk it down to experience, learn your lesson and don't be so obnoxious next time."

"Oh lighten up, you puritanical git. Who do you think you are, Mary Whitehouse?"

Bernard realised it was pointless trying to appeal to Ronnie's better nature. He didn't have one. All he knew was that he had to get Ronnie out of the drawing room before Abigail and Jocasta came in or all hell would break loose again.

"Come on, let's get back down to the cellar before they come in here. You've got your corkscrew now; you can crack open some wine."

"Now you're talking, my boy."

They left the drawing room and headed back to the cellar, just as the doorbell rang. As they closed the cellar door behind them, the modern version of Jamset appeared from the direction of the kitchens and headed for the front door to greet Abigail and Jocasta.

When they reached the cellar, Ronnie was distraught to discover that all the vintage bottles of wine had disappeared.

"We've been robbed! Where have they all gone?"

"Perhaps you drank them all when you got back to 1972?" suggested Bernard. "Or rather, you will drink them?"

"There were thousands of bottles down here, man. Even a man of my legendary drinking prowess couldn't have worked his way through all of those. And I once drank Jeffrey Bernard under the table at The Coach and Horses. Do you know what I think?"

"No, but I am sure you are going to tell me."

"I think you inherited the house and spent the whole of the next fifty years quaffing the lot."

"I don't drink. How many more times do I have to tell you?"

"For now, dear fellow, for now. But we all know it won't last."

"Whatever you say, Ronnie. If you're so keen to get your hands on that wine, let's get back down to the chamber and go back to 1972. Then you can have as much as you like. My treat."

"An excellent suggestion. Lead the way."

"In case there is anything scary?"

"Not at all, old chum. It's your house, therefore your place to lead. And as previously established, you are the one in possession of the torch."

Bernard took the torch from his pocket, switched it on, and they made their way down the secret passage. Fortunately, there was no need to search for a mechanism to activate it this time. The doorway to the passage was wide open. It seemed there was no longer any need to hide it in 2022. Why that might be, Bernard had no idea.

Before long they emerged back into the chamber, which was exactly as they had left it, with the five identical arches, flaming torches attached to the bluestone walls, and the ceremonial slab.

"Now then, all we need to do is go back through the arch from which we originally entered, and we're back in 1972," said Ronnie. "There's a bottle of Château Lafite in there with my name on it."

"Right you, are. Off you go, then."

"No, dear fellow, you lead the way. As I said in the cellar, you are the heir to all this, after all."

"Erm, well, the thing is, Ronnie…"

"You don't know which arch it is, do you?" said Ronnie, shaking his head in frustration at Bernard's incompetence.

"Well, they all look the same," replied Bernard.

Ronnie began wandering around the room looking at each arch in turn, to see if there were any distinguishing features.

"You're right. Damn and blast."

"Sorry, Ronnie. In all the confusion down here before, I kind of lost my bearings."

"Imbecile."

"Oh, be fair, Ronnie. You don't know which exit it is either."

"It's your house. Your responsibility. I have more important things to occupy my time with."

"Well, look, it doesn't matter. We'll just try one at random and see where it leads. If it's not right, we'll just come back and try another until we get the right one. Now then, which one did we just come through?"

"I don't know," replied Ronnie. "Weren't you paying attention?"

"Er, no, well, perhaps we should have stayed still rather than wandering around. I've lost my bearings now."

"You really are utterly useless! As usual, it will be down to me to make the important decisions. Come on, we'll go through this one."

Ronnie picked an arch at random and strode through it. Bernard followed figuring they had a one-in-five chance of getting it right. Those were reasonable odds, better than rolling a dice.

When they reached the cellar, Ronnie made his disappointment clear.

"Bloody hell! There's still no sign of the wine. You've picked the wrong bloody door."

"Wasn't it you that picked it?"

"Don't split hairs, Bernard. Come on, let's go back and pick another arch."

"Just hang on a minute. We may as well take a quick look upstairs just to clarify when or where we are."

"Why waste time doing that? We're obviously in the wrong place."

"Because I'm curious, that's why. And as you keep pointing out, it's my house. I lead and you follow, remember?"

"Very well. But I'll have you know I am doing this under protest."

Bernard led the way back up the steps until they emerged back into the house where they were astounded by what they saw.

They were most certainly not in 1972.

Chapter Seven
June 312

The house was unrecognisable; indeed, it became apparent very quickly that it wasn't even the same house. It didn't take them long to figure out that this time they had gone backwards in time – a long way back. Their opulent surroundings left them in little doubt as to the period of history they were now in. Both had not only seen but also acted in productions set in the era.

The room they had arrived in was built with fine white pillars set on mosaic floors. The walls were decorated with artwork depicting images of gladiatorial combat, whilst all around them, they could see statues showing naked women and men in various erotic positions. No theatre set they had ever been on had ever depicted a Roman villa as well as this, which was hardly surprising. They were looking at the real thing.

"Bloody hell, the house has changed a bit, hasn't it?" said Bernard. "It's like something out of a Bacchanalian orgy."

Ronnie's eyes lit up at this suggestion.

"An orgy, eh? Now you're talking. Did I ever tell you about the time I was backstage at the…"

"Yes!" said Bernard, interrupting. "And I don't want to hear about it again."

"Fair enough. But if there is an orgy going on here, I want in."

"I didn't say there was an orgy here, how would I know that? I just said all the erotic statues made it look a little Bacchanalian, that's all."

"Pity," said Ronnie. "Still you know the other thing the term Bacchanalian implies, don't you? Wine, and lots of it. Which is just as well bearing in mind the tragic disappearance of the vintage bottles in the cellar. Perhaps the Romans nipped down there and stole them. And now it's our job to liberate them!"

"That's jumping to conclusions, somewhat, isn't it?" replied Bernard. "You have a habit of doing that – usually the wrong ones."

"In your opinion perhaps, not mine. Anyway, there is bound to be some wine here somewhere, isn't there? The Romans were famed for it. You know I think I'm going to be right at home here. Better than 2022 and those moody-arsed women, that's for sure."

"Ronnie, you know nothing about Roman times other than what you've seen on *Up Pompeii!* do you?"

"I nearly had a part in the movie of that, you know, but I couldn't do it due to my commitments on *Sladen Street*. I must say it looked like an awful lot of fun. Apart from that bit with the volcano, obviously."

"I rest my case. I suppose you think Frankie Howerd is going to pop out from behind one of these pillars and start cracking dodgy double entendres at any moment, don't you?"

"Don't be silly, dear boy. I know more about this era than you think. I take it you didn't see my *Julius Caesar*, then?"

"You played Caesar?"

"Well, no, not him."

"Who, then? Brutus?"

"No."

"One of the senators? Third soldier on the right? A tree?"

"Shut up, Bernard."

"Hush a minute. I think someone's coming."

Heavy footsteps, made by the sound of a soldier's marching boots, were rapidly approaching. Bernard shoved Ronnie behind a statue displaying a rather well-endowed Roman emperor. He wasn't sure which one it was, but the sculptor had been extremely generous with the plaster in the nether regions.

He joined Ronnie behind the statue, only daring to sneak a peek around the corner once they were safely concealed. When he saw the outfit of the approaching figure it confirmed what they had already ascertained. They had indeed arrived in Roman times.

Bernard looked closer at the Roman officer who had just entered the room. He was dressed resplendently in red robes, headdress, and armour. He also sported an impressive array of medals, but it was his face that Bernard was most drawn to because he had seen it before.

"It's Jamset!" he whispered to Ronnie, behind him.

"What? That's impossible. That would make him about two thousand years old. Let me take a closer look."

Ronnie reached into his pocket, put on one of his many pairs of glasses, and peered around the edge of the statue at the latest incarnation of Jamset. Thankfully, he was not walking towards where they were concealed, but towards another door on the right-hand side of the room. This allowed Ronnie to observe him in profile without being spotted.

"My word, you're right, Bernard!" he exclaimed.

"Shush, he'll hear us," whispered Bernard, watching as a Roman centurion entered from the doorway that Jamset had been heading towards.

"Ah, Centurion, I have been looking for you," said Jamset. "Have you seen anyone unusual pass through here?"

"No, Commander. I also checked the wine store as you suggested, but there was nobody there."

Ronnie perked up at the mention of the wine store, giving Bernard an excited look.

"Very good. So, just to reiterate, you are keeping your eyes peeled for two men dressed in strange clothes. One is short and scruffy with too much hair. The other is taller and has no hair on top at all but vain as he is, he covers it up with a wig."

"Did you hear that impertinent cur! Every single hair on my head is a Rathbone original!" whispered Ronnie angrily.

"Really? I didn't know real hair came with dry cleaning instructions."

"Right, that's it," replied a furious Ronnie. "I've tried to be nice because of Diane, but it's time to put my military training to use. You need a damned good thrashing, my lad."

"Quiet, they'll hear you!" warned Bernard, but it was too late. Ronnie made a comically lame swing at Bernard, who easily moved out of the way. Unfortunately, his punch connected with the statue, causing it to topple forward. Bernard grabbed at it desperately to try to stop it from toppling to the floor but managed only to grab hold of the emperor's enormous penis which came off in his hand. The remainder of the statue fell to the tiled floor with a tremendous crash, instantly alerting Jamset and the centurion.

"There they are, after them, Hardknott!" cried Jamset.

"Yikes! Run for it!" yelled Ronnie, already haring up to a doorway at the rear of the hallway.

"Don't start going all *Scooby Doo* on me again!" shouted Bernard, as he set off after him.

Ronnie and Bernard exited via the door at the end of the room, hotly pursued by Jamset and Hardknott. They found themselves in a long corridor, but there was to be no escape that way. Their hearts sank as they clapped eyes on two more centurions at the far end. The only option available now was to take one of several side corridors leading off to the right.

They dived ninety degrees to their right into another long passageway, which was lined with doors on either side. Realising that they were probably not going to be able to outrun the soldiers who would surely know the layout of the house better than they did, Ronnie took the executive decision to try one of the doors at random.

"In here!" he shouted.

Bernard followed him in, taking a quick look back as he did. The soldiers hadn't yet turned into the corridor so they wouldn't know where they had gone for the moment.

It would buy them a little time. He slammed the door shut behind him and turned to take in their new surroundings.

They had arrived in a spacious circular room, the centrepiece of which was a large fire burning in a hearth in the centre of the room. Ronnie, however, was more interested in the six young women surrounding the fire, all of whom wore pristine white dresses.

Bernard could feel the heat from the fire, which he found a little surprising. It had been notably warm throughout the house and he had assumed that they had once again arrived on or around Midsummer's day. If that was so, what did they need this blazing fire for? Cooking? There was no sign of any utensils.

"Hello, and what do we have here?" enquired Ronnie, eagerly eyeing up their new acquaintances.

"Bloody hell, here we go again," said Bernard.

"Don't be alarmed, ladies. I mean you no harm. My name is Ronald Kitchener Rathbone. Both I, and my chubby chum here, are strolling players, hence our strange outfits."

Ronnie reached into his pocket and pulled out some breath freshener which he promptly sprayed into his mouth, filling the immediate area with a minty smell.

Bernard watched in complete bemusement. He had seen this routine many times before and it never worked. Why Ronnie persisted with it was beyond him. Strangely, though, on this occasion the women didn't recoil at Ronnie's presence like they usually did. Instead, they walked slowly towards him, with wide-eyed looks of curiosity on their faces. They couldn't have been more than about twenty years old.

One of them, who had long blonde hair which cascaded down around her shoulders, walked slightly ahead of the others. She had a more confident demeanour which suggested she might be their leader. She stopped a couple of yards in front of them and addressed them calmly.

"My name is Sextilia and we are Vestal Virgins," she began.

"Not for much longer, eh, Bernie boy?" said Ronnie. "This must be where the orgy's happening."

"Oh, for God's sake," said Bernard. "You never learn, do you?"

"Please do not interrupt, either of you," said Sextilia, sternly. "We are priestesses of Vesta, goddess of the hearth and this is our holy place. No man may enter here, under pain of death!"

"Death? That's a bit harsh, isn't it, just for taking a wrong turn," said Bernard.

"Those are the rules. We have taken a thirty-year vow of chastity to Vesta. Here, we tend her hearth and keep her flame burning."

"Is that why it's so bloody hot in here?" said Ronnie. "You want to put that fire out, it's ridiculous having that blazing away in the middle of summer. Tell you what, why don't we chuck a bit of water on it, and cool it down a bit? Is there a tap anywhere around here?"

"If you interfere with the hearth, the penalty is death."

"Well, this place is a laugh a minute, isn't it?" said Ronnie. "You'll be saying you don't drink next."

"Alcohol is forbidden!" said Sextilia. "The penalty is…"

"Let me guess, death?" said Ronnie.

"Correct."

"Why are men forbidden from entering here?" asked Bernard.

"Lest we be tempted," replied Sextilia. "Isn't that right, Cordelia?"

"I am afraid so," said another, dark-haired woman, who was impossibly beautiful, with curves that Ronnie could not tear his eyes away from.

"Well, I can see how temptation could be a big problem for you," said Ronnie, ogling the pair of them. "Especially when a man of my distinction enters the room."

There was a loud banging on the door from the soldiers, who had figured out that this was very likely where Ronnie and Bernard were holed up.

"We know you're in there. Come out right now!" shouted a voice that Ronnie recognised as that of Hardknott, the centurion who had been talking with Jamset earlier.

"No fear! Come in and get us!" replied Ronnie.

"You bloody idiot," said Bernard. "They know we're in here now!"

"They will not enter," stated Sextilia. "No man would dare enter our sacred area."

"I would," said Ronnie suggestively, turning his eyes back from the door and eyeing up Sextilia and the others again. He was behaving like a child in a sweet shop.

"Stop that, Ronnie," chided Bernard. "You sound like a dirty old man. If it hasn't escaped your notice, we've been condemned to death by these women as well as having a squad of highly trained Roman soldiers after us. Now can we please concentrate on the rather pressing matters at hand!"

"Speaking of pressing problems, I really ought to have paid a visit before we left the pub, but there don't seem to be any facilities in here. Listen, Sextilia, or whatever your name is, where's the Gents?"

"You speak strange words, old man. I do not understand."

"Less of the old if you don't mind. I'm looking for the water closet, but since you don't seem to have one, I'm going to have to come up with a contingency plan. Look, I know you're fond of this fire over here, but really, would it do any harm if I gave it a little watering? I'll just damp it down a bit, I won't put it out. Can't say fairer than that, can I?"

He turned towards the hearth reaching down to unzip his trousers to a gasp of horror from the assembled women.

"That is our sacred hearth!" exclaimed Sextilia. "Did you not hear what I said before? If you defile it the penalty is death!"

"Yes, but according to you, we've already been condemned due to our earlier transgression. So it doesn't make any difference what we do now. May as well be hung for a sheep as a lamb."

By now, he had unzipped his flies and was on the verge of pulling out his member.

"No, Ronnie!" exclaimed Bernard. "Put it away!"

Ronnie reluctantly complied, muttering something under his breath as he did.

"I don't suppose there's a back door out of this place, is there?" asked Bernard, hopefully. The banging on the door had ceased but they couldn't stay in the chamber forever.

"No, there is only one way out of here, the way you entered," said Cordelia.

"And you cannot leave anyway," added Sextilia. "You must die."

"Look, with all due respect, how are six puny women like you going to take down a man of my stature?" said Ronnie. "I don't see any weapons in here. What are you going to do? Shag me to death? Though, that wouldn't be a bad way to go, thinking about it. Not with this full bladder, though. Perhaps I could go over there, in the corner? I won't get a drop on your precious fire, I promise."

The banging on the door, having ceased temporarily, now resumed.

"Come out of there now!" shouted Hardknott through the door. "Stop hiding behind the skirts of women, and face us like men!"

"Bloody soldiers, spoiling my fun," grumbled Ronnie. "What's the plan, Bernard?"

"Me? Why are you asking me?"

"It's your house."

"No, it isn't. This isn't the same house. Mine won't be built for over a thousand years, yet."

"Fine, but you're the one who insisted we go off exploring, weren't you?"

"And you were the one who dragged us into this room. Didn't you look at the door first to see if there was a sign warning about death to all who enter? There is one, isn't there?" he asked, turning to Cordelia.

"We do not need one," she replied. "All men know not to come here. It is inscribed in the rules."

"Well, we didn't," said Ronnie. "You should have put it on the door, as Bernard said. I think we could claim innocence under the Trades Descriptions Act."

"I don't think that was around two thousand years ago, to be fair, Ronnie."

"Even so, bit harsh to kill us when we're new in town," said Ronnie. "Can't you just punish us a little bit? You could maybe spank me for a while and tell me not to be such a naughty boy. Seems like a reasonable compromise, don't you think?"

He sidled up towards Sextilia, hoping to appeal to her better nature.

"Even if these women were foolish enough to agree to such a dubious suggestion, it still doesn't solve the problem of the murderous soldiers outside, does it?" said Bernard.

"Believe me, those men outside are the least of your worries! We told you what fate awaited all those who entered here," said Sextilia.

"All a misunderstanding, my dear. Here, let me take your mind off it," said Ronnie.

"Ronnie, what the bloody hell do you think you are doing!" exclaimed Bernard, as Ronnie started stroking Sextilia's shoulder. Strangely, considering her earlier threats, she wasn't resisting but instead gazing deeply into his eyes with a look of lust on her face. What was going on here? They were meant to be chaste virgins, not seductresses. And who the hell would want to seduce Ronnie anyway? It didn't bear thinking about.

Ronnie failed to answer but just continued to gaze, mesmerised, into Sextilia's eyes. Bernard watched closely. There was something odd about this. He seemed unable to break the stare. It was as if she had him under a spell. Was this how these women were going to kill them, luring them in like a siren on the rocks?

He grabbed hold of Ronnie's arm, pulling him away from Sextilia and breaking his gaze in the process, but he was still seemingly under her influence.

"It's alright, Bernard. There is nothing to fear from these beautiful young vixens. All you need to do is succumb to their beauty and all our worries will be over."

"That's exactly what they want to happen! Don't you remember what they said? We have been condemned to death. I think this is how they do it. Take us into their power, then when we're helpless and smitten, stab us in the back or something."

"That's not true. Just look into her eyes, like I did. Then you'll understand."

Bernard tried to pull Ronnie away, but he refused to cooperate. All he wanted to do was gaze at Sextilia again. He brushed Bernard aside and looked back to her, the eyes so alluring, the body the most perfect he had ever seen. She leant towards him, offering him her lips. This was a dream come true. She did want him!

He moved in to meet her embrace, but the second their lips touched, she underwent a dramatic transformation.

Instantly she began to transform, her eyes bulging and turning red, glowing with fire. Her nostrils flared, and she opened her mouth revealing a forked tongue and fangs. Most terrifying of all, her hair took on a life of its own, rising and curling into a nest of snakes which twisted and writhed all around.

He pulled away, shocked, but not quickly enough as one of the snake heads spat a venomous, green liquid into his eyes. Instantly, he felt a burning sensation as the acidic poison began to sear his flesh.

"Gah! You poisonous bitch! She's blinded me. Do something, Bernard."

But Bernard could do nothing. He too was now paralysed. After his failed attempt to pull Ronnie away, he made eye contact with one of the other virgins and found that he couldn't break away, either. He was being drawn in, just as Ronnie had been. Would the same happen to him? Was she to transform into a venomous harpy too?

The situation was looking desperate, but then came a ghostly and timely intervention. The image of the old man that Bernard had seen outside the house earlier suddenly materialised in front of the hearth. He floated in the air, holding a flat palm out in front of him, just as he had before, like a policeman stopping traffic.

Whatever he was doing, it was working because as soon as he had appeared, the virgins became rooted to the spot. It was almost as if they were frozen in time, including the writhing snakes that had emerged from Sextilia's head. They were now motionless. Both Ronnie and Bernard found they were able to move again. They had been granted a temporary respite. Could they make use of it?

While all this had been going on, Hardknott and two other centurions had been deliberating their next move outside the door. Then a foot soldier arrived, carrying a large wax tablet.

"Thank you, soldier," said Hardknott, taking the heavy tablet which was at least two feet tall and a foot across. The top of the tablet was inscribed with the words 'Rules of the Vestal Virgins' with the list laid out underneath. Hardknott pored over the contents to see what their options were. After a moment or two, he had deciphered the information and come up with a plan.

"Right, so it doesn't say that we are not allowed to enter the chamber. All it says is that we are forbidden to gaze upon their beauty. So all we need to do is go in with our eyes closed, capture those two men, and come out again. Come on, lads. And remember to keep your eyes shut."

"How are we going to grab them, if we can't see them?" asked one of the soldiers.

"We'll get the virgins to direct us. They don't want those two in there any more than we do and will kill them if we don't get them out. My commanding officer wants us to capture them so he can interrogate them."

"But…" continued the soldier, who had spotted several flaws with the plan.

"No buts, now close your eyes and let's go."

They screwed their eyes tight shut and prepared to enter the chamber. After a small delay, while Hardknott was fumbling to find the door handle, they entered the room and wandered in. The ghost of the old man was still hovering over the hearth, but they couldn't see him or anything else. All four began stumbling around, crashing into and knocking over the statues.

The distraction was enough to break the ghost of the old man's temporary spell and he began to fade away. As he did so, the virgins began to move again, including the transformed creature that had once been Sextilia, which now let out a mighty roar. Startled, the soldiers opened their eyes.

"Sweet Isis! It's a monster!" exclaimed Hardknott. "Come on, lads, run for your lives!"

The three men panicked and ran back out of the door, hotly pursued by the creature who had, luckily for Ronnie, now decided they were a more attractive target than him.

"This is our chance to get away," exclaimed Bernard. "Come on, Ronnie! Can you see?"

To his relief, Ronnie felt his sight beginning to return. Whatever the creature had sprayed at him, it must have just been to stun him, so it could do whatever it had planned to do. Thankfully, the intervention of the soldiers had saved him.

"Just about. Stings a bit, though. What the hell was that thing?"

"It looked like a Gorgon," he replied. "But I thought they were part of Greek mythology, rather than Roman."

"Never mind where it's from. Let's get out of here before it comes back."

Bernard helped him up and they headed for the door, keen to get away as fast as possible. But Cordelia had other ideas and blocked their path.

"Where are you going?"

"Back to the chamber whence we came," said Bernard. "We need to get back to our own time, and fast."

"Yes, the chamber," said Cordelia dreamily. "I must go to the chamber. My destiny awaits me there."

"Your destiny?" asked Bernard. This was getting stranger by the minute. What did she know about all of this?

"It is the reason I came to this place. The truth is, I didn't want to become a Vestal Virgin. I'm not a virgin at all. I used to pull tricks for soldiers in the red-light district in Cirencester before I came here. But then I felt mysteriously drawn to this place. And, Bernard, I also feel a connection to you. It's almost as if we were linked in some way."

Never one to pass up an opportunity, Ronnie immediately intervened.

"Well, given your lax moral values, perhaps we should have a little fun before we go."

"Chance would be a fine thing. They've put this bloody chastity belt on me."

She gave them a quick flash under her dress revealing a belt containing an identical jewel to that which Jocasta had been wearing around her neck and which had also been on the amulet Bernard had picked up from the slab the first time they had entered the chamber.

"Look at that, Ronnie! It's that same jewel again. That's three times we've seen it now."

"Never mind that," said Ronnie. "She didn't say no, did you, my dear? You mean, you would consider it?"

He couldn't believe his luck. He would never admit it to Bernard, but since the end of his fifth marriage, his member had been largely resting, to use the acting terminology. The only action it had seen, he had been forced to pay for, which was something he would not want anyone else to know about.

"You're not bad for an old gent, I suppose," she conceded, much to his delight.

But then she spoiled it by adding, "Got any gold?"

So she was only in it for the money after all. It seemed things were no different here than they were in 1972. And for a moment there, he had deluded himself into thinking that she had genuinely liked him. But there was no time to dwell on that because the air was now being filled with a series of blood-curdling screams from afar, which were then suddenly cut off. The creature, which Bernard had identified as a Gorgon, had claimed at least one victim.

"We need to get out of here right now," said Bernard.

The three of them hurried out of the chamber, leaving the other four virgins behind. It was a timely intervention, as back in the drawing room, the Gorgon was standing over the dead bodies of the three centurions and the foot soldier.

Then she began to transform. But it wasn't back into the form of Sextilia. Instead, she changed to the form of the reaper-like figure that Bernard and Ronnie had encountered in the other time zones. The skeletal face gave a toothy grin of satisfaction at the killing that had just taken place, before pulling its hood down over its face and beginning to walk slowly back towards the hallway.

Meanwhile, Ronnie, Bernard and Cordelia were making their way back down the corridor towards the cellar door, when Ronnie noticed something on the floor.

"Have you noticed this mosaic on the floor, Bernard? There's a chap in it with a distinct look of you in the pattern."

He pulled out his pince-nez and bent down to take a closer look.

"Eh?" said Bernard, stopping and crouching down to examine the mosaic. "My goodness, you're right. And look here, this other chap is the spitting image of you. They've even got the wig right."

"How many times do I have to tell you, this is not a wig."

"How bizarre," said Bernard. "Why would they have images of us in the mosaic on the floor?"

"And look, here is one of you, Cordelia. And, Bernard, isn't this one of those frightful women from the future who threatened to call the bobbies on me?"

"It is. And look at this chap. He looks like a Cavalier from the Civil War."

"Didn't you claim you saw a ghost of a Cavalier in the cellar?"

"I did. But you didn't believe me."

"Sorry about that, old chap. A rare error of judgement on my part. Even I am not completely infallible. But after what I've just seen with that Gorgon thing, I'm willing to believe just about anything."

"Fascinating," said Bernard, looking at the various other images.

"Look, far be it from me to spoil this archaeological feast, but I think we should forget the mosaic and get a move on," said Ronnie. "That monster's probably going to be coming after us next!"

They moved on, though Bernard remained intrigued by what they had seen. How could their images appear on something created thousands of years before they were born? And what about the others, like Cordelia and Jocasta? What was the connection between them?

A few minutes later, the three of them emerged back through one of the arches into the chamber. Cordelia, who was seeing it for the first time, could barely contain her excitement.

"It's real! I have dreamt about this place so many times. This is where I was destined to come. But until today, I had no idea where to find it."

"Well, my dear lady, your destiny has arrived, and I am part of it," said Ronnie. "All we need to do is to walk through that arch there and within a few short hours, we can be drinking champagne in a swanky nightspot. And after that, back to my place."

"I thought your place was off limits for decoration," said Bernard.

"Yours, then."

He was still hopeful of taking advantage of the first woman in years to show interest in him. He was willing to overlook her admission to her former career as a sex worker in Cirencester. Admittedly, her request for gold had thrown him a little but then he had remembered some of the trinkets lying around the house in 1972 which were ripe for the taking. He was sure if he presented her with a few of those, she would gladly put out.

"No. I must go back to my sisters until the time is right for me to return here," said Cordelia, much to Ronnie's disappointment. "I cannot leave my own time. You must go with Bernard, back to where you belong."

"But what about the Gorgon?" asked Bernard. "It's not safe here."

"She only ever kills the male of the species. I have nothing to fear from her."

"Good," said Bernard. "Then, I think we're done here."

"Right, come on, let's go then," said Ronnie, resigned to the situation. "Perhaps we can catch up later, my dear, when all this nonsense is over, eh?"

"I would enjoy that," said Cordelia, much to Ronnie's delight.

"Excellent. Now then, Bernard, which arch is it?"

"Erm, well, the thing is, what with all the excitement, I've sort of..."

"You've forgotten again, haven't you? For Christ's sake. Right, I'm going to have to take charge of the situation. We'll try that one."

He began to walk towards one of the arches at random but Bernard stopped him.

"Hang on a moment. Before you blunder through any more doors, take hold of this."

Bernard reached into his pocket and produced a piece of chalk.

"Where did that come from?" asked Ronnie.

"I always keep a piece in my pocket. It's for when I'm playing darts in the pub. They never have any in The Feathers."

"Darts? Really. You are so working class, Bernard."

"Right, so what we need to do is mark the doors we've been through. Now, which ones can you remember?"

"Bernard, I have been drinking continuously since 1952. I can barely remember anything that has happened in the last decade, never mind the last hour. And as we have already established, you can't remember either. I bet you don't even know which one we just came out of."

"I can!" said Cordelia, enthusiastically. "We came through that one."

"Good," said Ronnie. "I'm glad somebody's been paying attention. Now, give me the chalk."

Bernard duly obliged, and Ronnie walked over to the arch that Cordelia had indicated.

"Now, my dear, tell me, what year is this exactly?"

"It is the year of the Consulship of Constantinus and Licinianus," replied Cordelia.

"That means bugger all to me," said Ronnie. "Pardon my French. Or do I mean Latin?"

"You know, I've been wondering about that," said Bernard. "How is it we're all speaking the same language?"

"Don't ask awkward questions, Bernard. Now how are we going to work out what year it is?"

"The Romans didn't measure years in our terms," said Bernard. "They named them or counted them from the date of the founding of Rome. We didn't start using the Anno Domini system until the sixth century."

"Never mind the history lesson," said Ronnie. "Listen, my dear, how long have the Romans been here in Britain?"

"Hundreds of years," replied Cordelia.

"Good enough, said Ronnie. "We don't need to know the exact year, do we? I'll take an educated guess."

He reached up and chalked the number 312 over the arch.

"Good," said Bernard. "And you know, now I come to think of it, I'm pretty sure that the one to the left of that must be 2022. It's all coming back to me now. I don't know why I couldn't remember before."

"Are you sure?" said Ronnie. "What about 1972?"

"Haven't a clue there, I'm afraid."

"Fine, we'll assume that one is 2022, for now," said Ronnie, chalking it over the door before looking at the others.

"You, know I reckon this one might be 1972, you know," he added.

"You just said you couldn't remember anything after 1952," said Bernard.

"It's true, I can't, but then it's only 312 now, isn't it?"

"That makes no sense whatsoever, but then nor does most of what you say. I suppose it's as good a guess as any. Are you sure you are going to be safe, Cordelia?"

"I shall return to my sisters, and prepare for my moment of destiny. At midnight, I shall return here."

"Excellent," said Ronnie. "See you at midnight, then! And bring a bottle in case we haven't found ours by then. Come on, Bernard."

And with that, Cordelia took the door marked 312, whilst Bernard and Ronnie headed through the unmarked arch which they hoped would lead to 1972.

Chapter Eight
June 1349

"This doesn't look like 1972 either," said Bernard.

"Agreed," remarked Ronnie. "I told you that you had chosen the wrong bloody arch again, but you wouldn't listen, would you?"

A weary Bernard couldn't be bothered to argue that it was Ronnie who had picked the arch. What was the point?

They had followed the passage from the archway up towards where they had expected the cellar to be, but there was nothing recognisable of the cellar at all this time, just a hollowed-out cave. It was still possible to continue onwards as there was a jagged, barely passable stone staircase leading up from the corner in the cave. It was in roughly the same place that the steps had been in the other time zones.

At this point, Ronnie had questioned the wisdom of proceeding any further. He had rightly pointed out that this was obviously not 1972, which was where they wanted to get to, so why bother? But Bernard was curious to see where the staircase led and ignored Ronnie's protests.

At the top of the stairs, they discovered a horizontal, square trapdoor directly above them. Bernard tried pushing it but could only get it to budge a fraction. It was as if there was something on top holding it down. Enlisting a reluctant Ronnie's help, he gave it an almighty heave and managed to get it to give way. Then they climbed out and surveyed their surroundings.

They were standing in a clearing in the middle of a forest. The trapdoor they had come through was now exposed, though it was very muddy and covered in some sort of mossy, green sludge where it had been buried under the forest floor. It didn't look as if it had been opened for a very long time. Presumably, that was the reason they had struggled so much to get it open.

"Where the hell are we now?" asked Ronnie. "Not only is there still no sign of my car but now we've lost the bloody house as well!"

"I'd hazard a guess we are still some time in the past before the house was built," replied Bernard, looking around pensively. "There's no sign of civilisation at all."

"And the Roman villa?"

"Abandoned and destroyed, I would imagine."

"I think you may be right," said Ronnie, examining some broken tiles on the ground nearby. "Look, there are some pieces of that mosaic here."

"Let's have a look," said Bernard, picking up a small broken piece of tile. "Oh, yes, look. I think this is a part of your wig."

"Don't start all that again. Come on, I suggest we go back through the trapdoor. There's no point hanging around here in the middle of nowhere."

"I don't think we should rush off just yet. I want to establish where and when we are first."

"Why? What's the point? There's no house, no booze, no nothing. It's a complete waste of time."

"Aren't you remotely interested in where we might be? I mean, look at the opportunity we've been given here. How many people get a chance to walk around in history?

This is the adventure of a lifetime and we should make the most of it."

"Admirable sentiments, my boy, but let's apply a little realism here."

"Realism? You? That's a laugh!"

"Bernard, I don't know what romanticised ideas you may have about history, but the truth is, most of it was smelly, horrible, and incredibly dangerous. Have you forgotten what happened in the last time zone? Marauding Romans and monsters? This could be even worse. What if we've arrived in Viking times? I don't want to end up getting raped and pillaged!"

"I don't think there's much danger of that," replied Bernard. "I'm not sure your average Viking warlord is partial to amorous encounters with balding middle-aged men."

"Your puerile jibes do not affect me. Hang around here and get hacked to death if you like, but I still say we should go back."

"Look, why don't we just walk through the woods for a bit and see if we can find the way to the village? We could ask at the pub what time we're in."

"Ah, you've tried that tack before, and I'm wise to your little game. Tempt him with the offer of the pub and he'll go along, eh? And do you think the pub will be there waiting for us in whatever godforsaken century this is?"

"It might be. Taverns are as old as the hills."

"And how, pray, are we to pay for any drinks we may be able to procure, assuming your mythical tavern exists? I highly doubt that our coins of the realm will be of any use here."

"What about those things you stole from the house earlier? Did you think I didn't notice?"

"Even I'm not desperate enough to swap 24-carat gold for a tankard of dodgy ale made from water out of some muddy stream."

"Maybe you can use your considerable charm to get someone to buy you a drink. It worked on Brian."

"It's highly unlikely that we are going to encounter any *Sladen Square* fans whenever this is, are we?"

"I'd have thought you'd have been glad about that. You're always banging on about how much you hate autograph hunters."

"True. I can see I am not going to persuade you from pursuing this foolhardy endeavour, so you had better lead on. Perhaps we can find some other way of blagging a drink."

They began to make their way through the very overgrown woods. They were far more difficult to traverse than they had been in 2022, and Ronnie was most perturbed when his waistcoat got snagged on some brambles. But eventually, they emerged to find a primitive village settlement in front of them.

However, what they saw was far removed from the congenial English village they had visited before. The muddy track that led towards the ramshackle collection of mud huts had been blocked by several large boulders. These were covered with crude chalked Xs and a sign warning to keep away.

"It doesn't look very friendly, does it?" remarked Ronnie.

To emphasise his point, an arrow whistled past his ear, grazing the side of his head. It wasn't enough to injure him, but it was enough to take his wig off, embedding it in a nearby tree trunk.

"Hahaha, I knew it!" said Bernard, creasing up with laughter at Ronnie's shock as his hands instinctively reached up to his now bald pate.

Ronnie was more concerned with restoring his dignity than responding to Bernard's mirth. He pulled the arrow from the tree, retrieving his hairpiece in the process. Then the voice of their unseen assailant rang out from somewhere behind the barricade of boulders.

"Plague carriers! Keep away!"

More arrows began to rain down around them. Bernard's jollity was quickly cut short as realisation overcame him that once again their lives were in danger.

"You bloody idiot!" shouted Ronnie. "I warned you something like this would happen! Come on, run for it!"

He replaced his wig and hot-footed it back into the woods behind them.

"Oh for heaven's sake. Run, run, run it's all we ever do!" yelled Bernard, following. He had done more running today than he probably had in the past ten years. It was exhausting, but he supposed it must be doing him some good. That was assuming he didn't end up with an arrow embedded in his back, of course. That would be very bad.

The run through the woods was even more haphazard this time. Before, they had been able to pick their way carefully, sidestepping brambles or stinging nettles. This time, under the threat of imminent death, there was no room for any of that. By the time they emerged into a small clearing, they looked as if they had been dragged backwards through the proverbial hedge.

"Stop a minute," said Bernard. "I need to rest."

"Where's the trapdoor?" asked Ronnie, in desperation.

"I don't think this is the same clearing."

"We're lost, aren't we? Well, thank you, Bernard, that's another fine mess you've got me into!"

"I can't hear anyone following. I think we're safe for the moment."

"What was that he was shouting? Something about plague carriers? That's a bit harsh. I haven't had a day's illness since I had measles as a kid."

"What? You called in sick to *Sladen Square* last Wednesday. I had to cover some of your lines."

"That wasn't exactly an illness. I bumped into George Best in a pub in Salford and he had a couple of Miss Worlds with him. One thing led to another, shall we say, and I found myself somewhat indisposed."

"I don't want to hear about it," replied Bernard, knowing that it was highly likely to be just one of Ronnie's fabrications. "Let's just concentrate on getting back to the house."

"What house? It's gone, remember?"

"In this time, yes. What I mean is let's just keep going back through the woods. We are bound to find the trapdoor back to the chamber eventually."

They were startled by crashing noises in the distance behind them in the woods. Then they heard a group of men chanting the same phrase repeatedly.

"Death to the plague carriers!"

"That's if the local lunatics don't get us first," said Ronnie. "So much for being safe. Everywhere you take us, we seem to have murderous swine hell-bent on carving us up. I told you we should have gone straight back, but no, you had to go off exploring, didn't you?"

"There's no time for recriminations now. We've got to keep going."

They blundered on through the woods, with the sound of the pursuing peasants getting ever louder.

"They're getting closer!" said Ronnie, beginning to panic. "What chance have we got against them? They'll know these woods far better than we do. Where's that bloody trapdoor?"

"Why are they following us if they think we've got the plague?" replied Bernard. "If they are so terrified of catching it they should be running away from us!"

"They are primitive peasants!" said Ronnie. "They lack the intellectual capacity to figure these things out in the way we educated twentieth-century folk can. Well, me, anyway."

Bernard didn't reply. He was becoming increasingly worried that they were going the wrong way but he couldn't admit that to Ronnie. He would never hear the last of it, assuming they survived.

Then he stopped abruptly, as they emerged into another small clearing. Standing right in front of them was an old man, dressed in tattered grey rags. Bernard recognised him straight away. He had seen him twice before, but both times he had been in a ghostly, incorporeal form. This time, he was solid and very much real.

"Follow me, quickly," said their new acquaintance. "We don't have much time."

Under the circumstances, they didn't need much persuading. It was either trust the old man or be murdered by the bloodthirsty locals.

They followed the aged man to the edge of the clearing, towards a strange cave-like structure. It was formed entirely from overhanging branches that had bent over and fused to form a makeshift shelter.

The pursuing pack had upped the stakes now, chanting "burn them, burn them!" as they stampeded through the woods. They couldn't have been more than twenty yards away by now.

"I don't know who this fellow is but if he stops us getting burnt at the stake by these nutters, it's good enough for me," said Ronnie.

"Right you are," said Bernard, who was right alongside him.

The cave was only about five feet tall, high enough for the diminutive old man but a little cramped for Bernard, who had to duck down. As for Ronnie, who was a good six feet tall, he had to practically dive inside to avoid being spotted by the angry horde who charged past just as they were safely out of sight.

Out of danger for the moment, they sat up and looked around the strange tree cave. It wasn't the most salubrious of dwellings, but at least it was safe. Bernard had no idea who the mysterious old man was, but he was grateful for the rescue.

"Thank you," he said. "That's the second time you've saved us. It was you, back in the Vestal Virgin chamber, wasn't it?"

"It was I," replied the old man.

"Well, we are very grateful. But please, do tell us, why are you helping us?"

"Because you are one of the chosen ones, my lord!"

Ronnie mistakenly attributed this address to himself and responded accordingly.

"Ah, you recognise a man of breeding when you see one! You are clearly a man of discernment, despite your somewhat shabby appearance. Rathbone's the name. Pleased to meet you. Though if I might offer a little advice, you ought to tidy this place up a bit. And yourself, come to that."

"You misunderstand, Mr Rathbone. When I said lord, I was referring to Mr Bradshaw here. Or to give him his correct title, Lord Blackwood, though I would advise you against adopting that nomenclature. Allow me to introduce myself. My name is Bateson."

"He's not a lord, he's a peasant," said Ronnie. "I am the one of noble birth, old man, not this stand-up comedian!"

"I am a seer and I see all things, Mr Rathbone. There is no noble blood in your lineage. Your paternal ancestor in this century is a dung collector from Hartlepool."

"That's an outrageous slur! You've just made that up. Bernard, I suggest you pay no attention to this charlatan."

Bateson was unperturbed by Ronnie's protestations and continued to speak in measured tones.

"On the contrary, from what I have observed of you, Mr Rathbone, it is you that has a penchant for making things up. I can assure you that Bernard here is of noble descent. I have been crossing the time fields to try to get your attention, but I could not communicate properly with you."

"I don't think he's a charlatan," said Bernard. "He has already shown us his powers. How else would he have held off the Gorgon? And before that, he tried to stop me from going back in the house."

"It is true, I do have powers, but I am old and I grow weary. My effectiveness is waning and I will soon pass on from this world. I have been trying to warn you and the others for centuries of the ancient evil that is awakening. But it has been to no avail, as alas you are now here and danger is close at hand."

"You don't look like a wise old seer to me," said Ronnie. "You look like some smelly old beggar. I mean, look at you. I've seen better clothes at C&A."

"Don't be so rude," said Bernard. "He knows a lot more about what's going on here than we do. Please elaborate further. What is this evil you been trying to warn us about?"

"It is why you were brought here, but I urge you not to take up your claim to the title of Lord Blackwood. It is a poisoned chalice, for sure. You are tainted by the blood of the demon Fendara. It means that you belong to the crooked line."

"What's the crooked line?" asked Bernard.

"It stems from your ancestor Fendara, a creature who lived long ago. He was possessed by an evil, ancient power. Terrible atrocities he did commit, terrible atrocities. You are part of his lineage."

"Hah! That puts my ancestor in Hartlepool into context then," said Ronnie. "At least he's earning an honest crust. For all you know, dung collector may be a perfectly respectable profession in this century. Speaking of which, when is this, exactly?"

"We are in the year of our Lord 1349," replied Bateson. "But the date is immaterial. Fendara's talons can transcend the linear nature of time. His agents will be here, searching for you, to ensure you are in the correct place at the appointed time."

"1349? That was the year of the Black Death, wasn't it?" asked Ronnie, feeling apprehensive.

"The very same," said Bateson. "That is why those men were chasing you. They will catch and burn any who approach the village."

"But that doesn't make any sense," said Bernard. "We were talking about this before. We heeded their warning and left the village when we saw we weren't welcome. If they thought that we were carrying the plague, why would they chase after us? Surely by touching us they would infect themselves?"

"I don't profess to understand the nature of their epidemic social distancing rituals," said Bateson. "All I know is they follow them religiously to the letter. If they catch you, they will burn you, but you will be safe here. They have not caught me yet."

"That's all very well," said Ronnie. "But I'm desperate for a wee. Can I do it inside? I mean it stinks in here already and there's what looks like dung all over the floor. You probably won't even notice."

"No, you must go outside," replied Bateson. "This is my home. I do not want a pool of your alcohol-fuelled urine on my floor."

"But what about the murderous peasants?"

"They've gone now. You'll be quite safe."

"Very well then," said Ronnie. "I could do with stretching my legs anyway. It's awfully cramped in here."

He crawled out of the cave and disappeared behind a nearby tree. With him out of the way, Bernard was able to quiz Bateson for more information, free of interruptions.

"While he's attending to his business, tell me more about this Fendara."

"He was a vile and wicked man. If he even was a man. Some say he was the devil incarnate, others that he was not of this earth. They executed him inside the stone circle near here, on the site of the house that will be built here in the future. The one you are in line to inherit. But the evil in him was powerful and his life force would not die. His body may have been destroyed but his consciousness transcended this realm and entered the spirit world."

"But if he is a spirit, how can he do anything?"

"He has the help of his human agents, those who believe in him and work tirelessly to return him to the physical world. He can also cast apparitions of himself across time, in the same way that I can."

"But why in my century? After so much time?"

"He can only wield his power for a day or so each year, on or around midsummer's day. At that time, the original five stones are in alignment with the sun. In addition, the planets must be aligned in a certain pattern. This is a rare occurrence, happening only five times in the three thousand years following Fendara's demise. This is one of those years, as is the one you came from."

"I know a little about astronomy. You mean like conjunctions between planets, or transits of Venus, that sort of thing?"

"Exactly. Each of the arches in the chamber leads to the years when the planets are aligned."

"And there is a chosen one like me in each one?"

"Indeed. The Fendara legend states that as he seeded his life force down the generations to his ancestors, he needs the blood from the five of you to reconstitute himself. Then he will return and take his revenge upon the world."

"I think I may have met some of the others. That girl Jocasta, in 2022, for one. So is another ancestor coming here?"

"Yes. He is coming here, very soon. I can sense his presence close by. I must try and dissuade him from going to the chamber. Just as you must not."

Ronnie stumbled back in, looking flushed and terrified.

"What's the matter?" asked Bernard. "The peasants haven't come back, have they?"

"A rash! I've got a rash! It's the plague."

"Really? Are you sure?" asked Bernard.

"Yes! I've just seen it. I've got the Black Death! I'm going to die!"

"You can't possibly have caught it that quickly. We've only been here twenty minutes."

"That's all it takes. Look at the state of him! He's probably crawling with germs."

"Where is this rash, exactly?"

"I'd rather not say."

"Why not? Come on, let's see it."

"No."

"Why not?"

"Because it's on my willy, OK? You don't want to see that, do you? Impressive though it is."

"No, I don't. We saw enough of it at the Christmas party last year. What sort of rash?"

"Just sort of red, and inflamed. With a couple of blisters."

"Yes, now I think I know what's happened here. This business with these Miss Worlds last week. What exactly went on?"

"Well, er, a gentleman never kisses and tells, you know."

"You do. All the time."

Ronnie had no intention of telling Bernard that there was nothing to kiss and tell about, at least where George Best and beauty contest winners were concerned. He had made all that up and there was no way he was going to admit to what had actually occurred.

He had been cruising along at five miles per hour in the Jensen outside Piccadilly Station, looking for a phone box, when he had been approached by a streetwalker. It wasn't his fault. It had been a moment of weakness and could have happened to anyone. He didn't want anyone finding out, though, so he would bluff his way through it as usual.

"Listen, dear boy, since you split up with Diane you've been a frightful bore. By regaling you with tales of my amorous adventures, I'm encouraging you to get back out there and enjoy some encounters of your own."

"No thank you. I don't go with just anyone. It's blatantly obvious what's going on here. You've caught the bloody pox, mate. We'll get you some antibiotics when we get back to 1972."

Bateson had been listening patiently to the exchange, and now that Ronnie no longer believed he was dying of the plague, he was finally able to get a word in edgeways.

"Do not preoccupy yourself with these trivialities, my lord. There is much to be done."

"By whom?"

"By you."

"By me? What can I do?"

"More than you know. You are a good man. You do not feel that you are because of recent events, and you do not believe you can be strong on your own. You still believe that you need the love of another. But you do not. It is time to draw on your inner strength and fight, not just for your future, but that of the whole world."

"You're right about that," said Ronnie. "He's been bloody hopeless since his wife left him. It's all Diane this and Diane that. He just can't let it go, no matter how many times he's told."

"I can't help that," said Bernard. "I can't control how I feel."

"You must put all that behind you," said Bateson. "You will soon face great peril."

"We've already faced great peril!" exclaimed Ronnie. Why do you think we're hiding out in this glorified toilet? We didn't pop in to admire the furnishings."

"Ignore the babblings of your foolish friend, my lord. His life will soon be in mortal danger. You will do anything to save him, even at the risk of your own. That is just one example of the virtuous hero that you shall become."

"Him, a hero?" exclaimed Ronnie. "Don't make me laugh."

Bateson gave Ronnie a withering look and said, "He is a hero. He just doesn't know it yet."

"What about me?" asked Ronnie hopefully. "A future Oscar winner? A knighthood? Tell me, oh wise seer, what does the world have in store for the legendary Ronnie Rathbone?"

"You, Mr Rathbone, have no redeeming features whatsoever. A life of obscure mediocrity is all that awaits you."

"Whatever you say, old man. I'd stick to writing horoscopes for the fourteenth-century equivalent of the *Daily Mirror* if I were you. That's if you can write, of course, which is a big assumption."

They were disturbed by the sound of a horse's hooves approaching from the woods, accompanied by a neigh.

"There's someone out there," said Bernard.

"It will be him, the one they call the Stranger," said Bateson. "He is Fendara's leading agent and is the one most instrumental in bringing about his return."

"What does he look like?" asked Bernard.

"He takes the image of the Grim Reaper."

"I thought so. That's why I asked. I've seen him. Several times. So did Ronnie, once, but he ran away."

"He will be coming for me," said Bateson. "You had better make haste in your escape."

"You could come with us."

"I cannot leave this place. I must be here to warn your ancestor. I will try to evade my enemy here, but you must return to 1972 and find a way to defeat Fendara. Warn the others from your bloodline and above all, do not go to the chamber at midnight. Now, go. Straight ahead from the entrance here, for thirty yards, and you will find the tunnel that leads back underground."

"Thank you for everything, Bateson," said Bernard.

Ronnie said nothing, just cast a disparaging look in Bateson's direction before the two of them scampered away into the woods, just before the Stranger rode into the clearing aboard a black stallion. The horse let out another loud neigh as it came to a halt and its rider dismounted. His appearance was, as ever, that of the Grim Reaper. The only thing missing was his scythe, which presumably was awkward to carry on a horse.

He tethered his mount to a tree, walked across the clearing, stood directly in front of Bateson's cave and began speaking.

"Come out, old man. I know you are in there. Come out or I shall burn your dismal dwelling to the ground."

The old seer emerged from the cave and stood in front of his enemy. He knew that he was doomed; he had already foreseen it. But he would have his say before he met his Maker.

"You shall not triumph, Stranger. Before your arrival, I met Fendara's descendant from 1972 and told him everything. He will no longer go to the chamber as you had planned."

"You disappoint me, Bateson. But your interference will do no good. Warning those fools won't make any difference. When the time comes, the children of Fendara will fulfil their destiny. They will have no choice and then he will return."

"Maybe he will, maybe he won't. But I do know that you won't win. Evil will be defeated, like it always has been since the dawn of time. Young Bernard is a hero in the making, even if he does not know it yet. He shall defeat you."

"A touching speech, old man, but a hollow one. Fendara shall return. Sadly, you will not be around to greet him."

The Stranger extended a long bony figure at Bateson, and a bolt of lightning shot out, immediately reducing the old seer to a smoking pile of dust. He smiled at a job well done and turned back towards his stallion, just as a well-dressed young man emerged from the woods.

The Stranger quickly hid his skeletal features beneath his cloak, not wishing to alarm the new arrival, who spoke to introduce himself.

"Excuse me, good sir. My name is Samuel Blackwood and I am a merchant from London. I received a message requesting me to report to this exact location at this time."

"But of course, Mr Blackwood. It was I who sent for you. I am pleased to tell you that a glittering inheritance awaits you. Allow me to give you this gift as proof of my credentials."

The Stranger handed over a solid gold bracelet encrusted with the same red jewel that had come into the possession of all the other children of Fendara. His hand was now gloved, and his arm was covered in a sleeve, disguising his true nature. This hadn't been the case just a minute before when he had despatched Bateson, but he had many powers. The ability to transform his appearance was one of them.

"Now, if you'd like to follow me," he said, as he began to lead the new arrival through the woods.

"Thank you," said Samuel, somewhat tentatively. This meeting was highly irregular, and he had doubted the wisdom of coming along. It wasn't something he would normally do, but he felt strangely drawn to the place. He had already received ample compensation with the jewelled bracelet. As a jewellery trader, he could see right away that it was worth a fortune. He tucked it away in his pocket and followed the Stranger through the woods.

When the Stranger stopped and lifted a large, square trap door embedded in the forest floor, he felt some reservations. What was he letting himself in for? Was it safe? But then he felt a reassuring thought in his head. Of course, there was nothing to fear.

"This way, my lord," said the Stranger. "That jewel I gave you is but a mere hors d'oeuvre to the glittering fortune that awaits down here."

Any lingering doubts Samuel had been feeling faded away. His newfound companion had no intention of killing him. If it had meant him harm, it would have done so already. And if there were riches down here beyond his wildest dreams he would be crazy to walk away. He would be wondering for the rest of his life what might have been. What did he have to lose, especially in these plague-ridden times? He could be dead at any moment. The risk was worth taking.

Slowly, he began to descend the jagged stone steps that led below the ground.

Chapter Nine
June 1645

Almost three centuries after Bateson's death, Samuel Blackwood's descendant, Thomas, was just arriving home at the newly built Fendara's Lodge. Dressed flamboyantly in the style of a seventeenth-century Cavalier, he cut a dashing figure in his long flowing cloak and a wide-brimmed hat.

He was a strong young man, and he flung the large doorway open with ease before striding into the hallway. There, the ever-present Jamset was waiting for him.

"Welcome home, Lord Blackwood. What news of the war?"

"I regret that it is not going well. We engaged with the enemy at Naseby in Northamptonshire but suffered heavy losses. At one point, when a Roundhead was standing over me, sword drawn, I did not think I would live to see another dawn."

"But you managed to escape, my lord?"

"I'm here, aren't I? You know, the strangest thing happened. He was about to run me through with his sword when I swear the Grim Reaper himself did appear to me. Of course, I assumed he had come because it was time for me to meet my maker. But then he fired a bolt of lightning at the Roundhead and struck him down. It seemed the Reaper had come for him, not me. After that, I managed to get away, but it wasn't easy to get back to Shroudshire undetected."

"I take it that you received my message?"

"I did. It was passed to me three days ago in Warwick. I must confess I found the contents somewhat perplexing. An urgent summons home, to be here no later than Midsummer's day, with no explanation. Now, what is all this about?"

"I was acting on instructions from the King himself. He is sending forces to rendezvous with you here tomorrow. You must defend the house against Cromwell's forces, who will be gathering tomorrow at the tower on the other side of the woods. I could not give the details to the messenger lest it fall into enemy hands."

"Very well. You did the right thing. We must remain vigilant. The enemy has agents everywhere and we cannot be sure who we can and cannot trust. Now, I require refreshment after my long journey. Please fetch me some wine."

Jamset left the room, leaving Thomas to relax. For now, he was safe back in his familiar home surroundings but if the enemy was coming here, the house might not be safe for much longer.

The room was luxuriously furnished, and immaculate. It was the same room that Ronnie and Bernard had found sorely in need of refurbishment hundreds of years later. But now, in 1645, it was resplendent, having been built just a few years before. Thomas was pleased to see that it had been kept spotless in his absence. He had not been home for many months.

Everything was where it should have been, apart from one mysterious item that caught his eye. Since his last visit home, someone had placed a large silver chalice on the mantelpiece, which was encrusted with a bright red jewel. Where had it come from? At twenty-five years old, he was not yet married, and both his parents had died relatively young. Other than Jamset and the other servants, he lived alone in the house.

Curious, he wandered over to the mantelpiece to take a closer look. He picked it up, running his finger over the jewel. Was it a ruby? It certainly looked like one. There was something most alluring about it and he didn't want to put it down.

Then Bernard and Ronnie walked in, dressed in their twentieth-century clothes, which by now were extremely bedraggled. It was unprecedented for people to walk in unannounced in this way and with everything that was going on, he automatically challenged them.

"I say, you two! Who are you and what are you doing in my house?"

"Us?" replied Ronnie. "Oh, we're just passing through, ignore us. You've chosen the wrong arch again, Bernard. This isn't 1972."

"You chose the arch," replied Bernard. "You always choose it, and then try and blame me when you get it wrong. Do forgive us, kind sir, we'll just be on our way. Forget we were ever here."

But Thomas was having none of it.

"Oh, no, you don't! You're Roundhead spies, aren't you? Hold it right there!"

Thomas turned and grabbed a large musket that was mounted on the wall behind him, before turning back and brandishing it at them.

"Bloody hell, look at the size of that thing!" exclaimed Bernard.

"If I had a pound for every time a woman's said that to me, I'd be able to buy this house myself," replied Ronnie.

"This is no time for your fantasies," said Bernard. "We need to get out of here."

"Agreed," replied Ronnie. He began to edge back towards the door but tripped and fell over a footstool. As he hit the floor, his wig, which he had only loosely reattached after the incident with the arrow, fell off again, exposing his bald patch. He hurriedly grabbed at his hairpiece to try to put it back on but Thomas had seen his bald, round head and jumped to the obvious conclusion.

"I knew it! You are a Roundhead. Well, you're going to feel the full force of my musket, you traitorous swine."

"Run!" yelled Ronnie, scrambling to his feet, and making for the drawing-room door, with Bernard not far behind him. Once again, in his panicked state, he wasn't thinking clearly. When he reached the hallway he headed towards the front door rather than the cellar.

"Not that way!" yelled Bernard, to no avail. Ronnie was already out through the door and making for woods. Bernard followed, cursing the idiocy of the man. Hadn't he learnt his lesson the last time he had blundered into those woods? Now they were going to be stuck in another time zone. And he was already feeling knackered.

"Bloody running!" he exclaimed, between breaths. "We're always bloody running!"

They reached the trees, just before Thomas fired the musket from the front door. It left a smoking hole in a tree, barely a foot to the right of Bernard's head, as they reached the cover of the woods. For the moment, at least, they were safe.

There was no one in the woods as far as they could see. But in almost the same spot, over three hundred years in the future, Ken was still watching the house, which was all quiet. He was alone, as Charlie had gone back into the village again to use the telephone box to report on progress.

In his luxury pad in Manchester, the Colonel was lying face down on a black leather couch, being treated to a luxurious massage by his Thai visitor when the phone rang. The masseuse passed him the telephone which he answered in his usual manner before Charlie began to fill him in with the latest news.

"I haven't seen Rathbone and his little friend in a while, but there was an Indian fella busy carrying stuff into the big house earlier."

"Trivia, Charlie, trivia. You've nothing to report at all have you?"

"But you did say to keep you informed."

"Hmm. That Rathbone's a slippery customer and I'm sure he's up to something but you're not going to find anything out hanging around outside the house, are you? If they aren't going to come out, you'll have to go in."

"How am I going to do that?"

"I don't know, do I? I'm not there. That's what I pay you for. Why don't you knock on the door and tell them you've come to read the gas meter or something? You look the type."

"A gasman? At this time of night?"

"You're in the countryside, tell them you were held up by a herd of passing cows or something. Use your initiative, man. And don't phone me again tonight unless it's important. I have far more pressing matters to attend to. Goodnight."

The Colonel leant over and replaced the handset, as the Thai girl continued her soothing ministrations on his back.

"Aah, that's lovely, my dear. Now then, are you ready for me to turn over?"

She signalled her approval, and he rolled over. This was his favourite bit. And what made it all the sweeter was that it was being paid for by mugs like Ronnie.

Meanwhile, Ronnie and Bernard were once again lost in the woods. At least it was sunny and warm this time and there were some clearly defined paths to follow.

"I don't see the point of tramping around in these woods again," complained Ronnie.

"Perhaps you should have thought about that before running out here again. How are we meant to get back to the house now with that Cavalier waving his musket about? He nearly took my head off with it a few minutes ago."

"Maybe we can find that trapdoor again?" suggested Ronnie.

"I doubt it. I think that the house was built over it."

"Yes, but it was all woods? How can you build a house there?"

"Half the country was wooded at one time. Things can change a lot in three hundred years. Perhaps it was cleared for agriculture. By the way, that Cavalier? He was the same one I saw in the cellar. And the mosaic. I think he's another member of the crooked line."

But Ronnie wasn't listening. They had emerged into a large meadow which was full of wildflowers, not that Ronnie had noticed them. His eye had been drawn by a group of three young women, dressed in chaste, white dresses, busy picking the flowers.

"I say," began Ronnie.

"Don't even think about it," snapped Bernard, determined to stop Ronnie before he said something inappropriate.

Ronnie was about to commence his patter in defiance of Bernard, but then remembered that his appearance might leave something to be desired. He adjusted his wig, tried to brush some of the foliage off his clothes and gave his armpits a quick sniff. They didn't smell too clever after all the running but maybe that wouldn't matter too much in this century. He couldn't imagine that the locals went around smelling of roses.

"It has to be said, travelling to these different time zones does have its compensations, dear boy," he said to Bernard. "I'll just introduce myself to these young ladies over here. It would be rude not to."

"It might also be extremely foolish," said Bernard. "Remember what happened to the last girl you tried it on with? She turned into a Gorgon!"

Ronnie ignored him and made a beeline for the girls, but before he reached them, the Stranger emerged out of the woods on his black stallion. In a sweeping move, he grabbed Ronnie and hauled him over the back of the horse with impossible ease. There was no way he ought to have been able to scoop up a man of Ronnie's stature that easily. It led Bernard to suspect that his abductor must have superhuman strength.

Ronnie found himself quite unable to move, pinned down by the Stranger's skeletal right arm as he steered the horse back into the woods with the other. All he could do was utter a brief cry for help before he disappeared.

"Bernard! Help me, man!"

And then he was gone. Bernard did not even attempt a pursuit. It was completely pointless. He couldn't outrun a horse. He could barely run at all as had been all too painfully proven over the past few hours. Instead he decided to ask the young ladies, who had been watching in bemusement, for some advice.

"Good evening. I wonder if you could help me. I'm afraid that everywhere we go, my friend gets himself into trouble and as you just saw, he's gone and got himself captured. I'm not too familiar with the local area and I was wondering if you could tell me where that path leads?"

"That is the way to the tower, sir. Maybe they are taking him there," said one of the girls. "That is where they keep the prisoners."

"Thank you," said Bernard. "You've been very helpful.

He followed the path, as the light began to fade from the sky. He felt tired. His body clock must be all over the place with all this leaping around in time. It didn't help that it was dark one minute, light the next, and then dark again. If there was a time travel equivalent of jet lag, his current state of exhaustion was surely it. How many hours had it been since they had first arrived at the house? Six? Ten? He had completely lost track.

He hurried on, keen to be out of the woods before it was completely dark. He knew from experience that it wasn't a pleasant place to be at night. He thought about the girls in the clearing, just picking flowers. It seemed an odd thing to be doing so close to sunset. Had they been put there deliberately to lure Ronnie out into the open? But why would the Stranger do that, with the powers he possessed? If he wanted to capture them or do them harm he could have done so at any time.

He couldn't imagine that rescuing Ronnie was going to be an easy task, and what he saw when he emerged from the woods confirmed that. About a hundred yards ahead of him was a circular tower, which was shaped similarly to a lighthouse. It was tapered such that it was somewhat wider at the bottom than at the top, which sported the traditional battlements you would expect to see on the turret of a castle.

It wasn't the battlements that concerned Bernard, though, it was the two Roundhead guards on either side of the front door. He could also see the Stranger's horse tethered up outside. If the girl in the forest was correct, that was where Ronnie had been taken. So what was he going to do to get him out?

He thought about what Bateson had said about him becoming a hero. He had said that he would have to rescue Ronnie soon. The old seer had been right. But how was he going to do it? He looked over at the two guards and mulled over the situation. He needed to come up with a plan.

Ronnie had indeed been taken into the tower where the Stranger had dragged him, complaining all the way, down the circular stone steps that led to the dungeons below. There, he flung him to the floor of a cell which was covered in straw and mud. By now, Ronnie had recovered from shock at being captured, and had reverted to his usual haughty manner.

"How dare you treat me this way you impudent dog, I'll have you know…"

"Quiet, imbecile. I have had enough of your inane chatter on the way here. Trying to convince me that you are going to be late for the BAFTAs indeed."

"I am! They're tonight and I must be there to receive my prize!"

"I know all about you, Mr Rathbone, and I know that you have never been nominated for a BAFTA, and you never will."

"I bloody ought to be, but they are rigged against me. It's because I'm on ITV you see. Now if *Sladen Square* were on BBC1 it would be a different matter. Then they would give me the credit I so richly deserve."

"Is there no end to your ceaseless prattling? I wonder how long you can keep it up in the room of eternity."

"Eternity? You should get Bernard in here. He's been bleating on about his ex for what seems like an eternity. You'll be desperate to let us go after a few hours of listening to his maudlin ramblings."

"You think I speak in jest? This room is outside of time. You could be in here for a thousand years and not one second will have passed outside. It will be forever Midsummer's day, 1645, for you."

"If that is indeed the case, my good fellow, you had better go and rustle me up an eternal bottle of brandy. I'll need some sustenance to see me through the aeons, won't I?"

"You do not seem to be taking me very seriously, Mr Rathbone. Not that it matters, as you are of little importance in the grand scheme of things. Your friend, on the other hand, is vital to my plans. Soon he will be here to try and rescue you, though why he should be so loyal considering the way you treat him is beyond me."

"Well, I hope he hurries up. Even his company is preferable to yours."

Outside, Bernard was still trying to figure out a way to get past the guards. He had managed to get closer to the tower without being seen by sneaking around the edge of the woods and then coming in at right angles to the front door. It was fully dark now, which helped. Now he was creeping from tree to tree but had gone about as far as he dared. What next?

The entrance to the tower was an arch-shaped door, not dissimilar to the arches they had found in the cellar. It was illuminated by two flaming torches which gave him a chance to get a good look at the guards. He could see that they were hefty types. However, given the level of education in this era, he didn't imagine they would be particularly bright. He was no Einstein, himself, but even so, surely his twentieth-century brains could beat their seventeenth-century brawn.

He rummaged through his pockets. What could he find to blind them with modern science? Of course – he still had the torch that he had found in the cellar earlier. Inching around the side of the tree, he switched it on and shone it onto another tree, directly in the line of sight of the guards.

"Ere, Fred, there be a strange light shining on that tree," said the guard on the left. He had an incredibly strong rural accent. Had Ronnie been here, he would no doubt have denounced him as a country bumpkin."

"What's that then, Bill?" replied Fred, in a similar accent.

Bernard watched with amusement. He had been right. These guards sounded, for want of a better word, thick. He moved the torch across the ground so it looked as if it was coming after the men, then shone it directly onto Fred's armour.

"Fred, look out! That weird shiny light! It's attacking you!"

"Argh! Argh! Get it off me."

Bill drew his sword and attempted to swat the light, almost impaling Fred in the process. Then Bernard, who was enjoying the spectacle tremendously, switched the light over onto him.

"It's trying to get me now!" shouted Bill. "What witchcraft is this?"

Bernard decided to take a chance. If these guards were as dumb as they seemed they would probably also be superstitious. He just had to hope that they had heard of the legend of Fendara. It was possible considering the number of references they had seen to him – from the name of the house to the local ale. He adopted a deep, booming voice, and shouted out as loudly as he could.

"Bill! Fred! This is Fendara speaking. I have come to cast judgement on you for your sins."

"What sins?" asked Fred. "I have not sinned."

"He must mean Molly in the milk shed," said Bill.

"Shut up. I told you what happened. We spilt some milk, that was all."

"No it wasn't," called out Bernard. "I know all about what you and Molly got up to, Fred, you naughty boy."

He was wondering if he was going too far. He was hamming this up like he was performing in a pantomime. No one in his world would possibly be stupid enough to fall for this routine. But it seemed to be working here.

"It must be Fendara!" exclaimed Fred. "They say he can see all."

"That's right, I do, and I know all about what you've been up to as well, Bill," shouted out Bernard.

"You don't mean that business with the candles, do you?" said Bill, nervously.

"Yes, Bill. You dirty boy. But if you do as I say, I shall absolve you of your sins."

"What must we do, oh mighty Fendara?" asked Bill.

"Go home immediately, and say the Lord's Prayer five hundred times. Then you may return here and we shall say no more about it."

"That we shall, sire, that we shall. Please forgive us our sins," begged Fred.

"Very good, off you go then."

The two guards hurried off, almost falling over in their heavy armour in their desperation to get home. Bernard couldn't believe how easy it had been.

"Blimey, that was a doddle," he remarked, chuckling to himself. "I've seen brighter folk in Runcorn."

The guards had departed in such haste that they hadn't even thought to secure the door to the tower. It was wide open, so Bernard emerged from behind the tree and made his way towards it. Unfortunately, all his efforts to trick the guards had been in vain. Just as he arrived at the archway, he felt a bony hand grab his shoulder.

Even through his clothing, the grip felt icy to the touch. He wheeled around to see the Stranger. He was still devoid of his trademark scythe but that was of no comfort, as he had upgraded it to a musket, which he was now pointing right at him.

The Stranger took his hand from his shoulder and lifted his hood, revealing his skeletal features. Although Bernard had seen him several times before, it had never been up this close and he recoiled at the image before him.

"Not so fast, Mr Bradshaw. You might have fooled those idiots, but you don't fool me."

"Bugger," said Bernard, which was the only word that came to mind. This wasn't looking too clever. And he had been so pleased with the way he had tricked Bill and Fred. So much for being a hero.

Inside the tower, Ronnie had curled himself up into a ball and retreated into the corner of the cell. Many hours had passed for him, despite it only being a few minutes outside. He was beginning to appreciate what the Stranger had meant when he called it the room of eternity. Now he was holding his hands folded across his chest in search of some sort of comfort. For all his bravado in the face of the enemy, he was in reality scared stiff.

Then the cell door opened, and he looked up to see Bernard walking in. The despair vanished from his face to be replaced by a look of joy.

"Bernard! You've come to rescue me. Bateson was right! You are a hero! I knew you wouldn't let me down."

His look of joy was short-lived as the Stranger followed Bernard into the room, holding the musket.

"I am sorry to disappoint you, Mr Rathbone, but there is to be no rescue," said the Stranger.

"Bollocks," said Ronnie.

"I have, however, brought your little playmate. I do hope you two are going to enjoy eternity together."

"Eternity?" asked Bernard. "I don't like the sound of that."

"Neither would I if I were in your unfortunate position. Mr Rathbone here was only telling me earlier how he was hoping to hear more about you and your ex. Well, you now have all the time in the universe to go over it in painstaking detail – again and again, and again."

"Oh no, spare me," said Ronnie.

The Stranger cackled manically and left the room, slamming the door behind him. Ronnie's brief hopes of rescue had been well and truly quashed and he wasted no time in making his feelings known.

"You blithering idiot! You were supposed to be rescuing me. Instead, you've gone and got yourself captured too."

Bernard was in no mood for any of Ronnie's nonsense. It was high time he stood up for himself. He had been allowing him to belittle him for far too long.

"Oh shut up, you pompous buffoon. You were the one stupid enough to get captured in the first place. If you'd not run off outside we'd be back in 1972 by now."

"Hardly. You're the one that got us into this in the first place by inheriting the house. So it's all your fault."

"Look, there's no point in us trying to apportion blame, is there? We're in this together. It isn't just some jolly adventure anymore. You heard what Bateson said. The fate of the whole world, not to mention us, lies in the balance."

"And you believe in the ramblings of an old git who lives in a hut made of sticks and dung, do you? Even if what he said was true, I can't say I fancy my chances if it's down to you to save the world. Let's face it, you couldn't save your marriage, could you? That's why Diane ran off with one of the crew."

This insult was the final straw that broke the proverbial camel's back. Bernard was furious, and bent down to where Ronnie was still lounging in the corner of the cell floor and grabbed him around the neck.

"You've pushed me too far this time, Ronnie. I could bloody strangle you right now, I honestly could."

The cell door opened and the Stranger came back in.

"Well, well, three minutes and you're already trying to kill each other. Eternity will just fly by."

"Why do you keep going on about eternity?" asked Bernard, relaxing his grip on Ronnie. "

"Oh, didn't your friend tell you? Time does not pass at the same rate here. Seconds in the outside world can be millennia in here."

"He's right," said Ronnie. "I've been here hours. That's why I ordered some booze off this bony-arsed fellow here to help us while away the time. Sadly, he hasn't come through with it yet. You know, from an imbibing point of view, I'm finding this so-called adventure increasingly disappointing."

"Yes, but we're supposed to be back at the house by midnight," said Bernard.

"You clearly don't understand, so let me spell it out again," said the Stranger. "Time does not pass in here as it does in the outside world. So, once I've let you rot in here for, oh I don't know, say ten thousand years, I'll then come and get you for the ceremony in the chamber. You'll be begging for Fendara to take your life force by then."

"I'll never give in to Fendara," said Bernard, determinedly.

"That's the spirit," said Ronnie. "You see, you do have some spunk after all. Just like Bateson said you did. Why do you think I was winding you up about Diane just now? I was trying to help you get your dander up. You can be a hero, my boy, you still can."

"Speaking of spirits," said the Stranger, "I believe you placed an order, Mr Rathbone."

He clicked his fingers, and some crates materialised in the middle of the cell.

"I mean, if you're going to spend ten thousand years in here, why spend it sober?" he added.

"By Jove, he's come through," said Ronnie, who had leapt to his feet and gone over to examine the crates. "This one's full of rum! I'd have preferred brandy, but beggars can't be choosers."

"And, for you, Mr Bradshaw, a few cases of Wood Pit bitter. I understand it's your favourite. Go on, tuck in. It's going to be a very long night."

And with that, the Stranger once again left the room, roaring manically.

"I wish he wouldn't keep coming in and out and laughing like that," said Ronnie. "It's like the worst, hammiest actor you can imagine."

"I don't need to imagine him, I'm looking at him," said Bernard, who was not sure what to do next. He knew what the Stranger's game was. He was trying to tempt him with the booze, to break his spirit.

"Never mind, let's just have a drink, eh? Oh, bugger, there are no glasses. Still, what does it matter? Straight from the bottle will do, eh?"

"You shouldn't tempt me, Ronnie. It was hard enough staying on the wagon after Diane left me but even that pales into significance against the thought of having to spend millions of years in here with you."

Then an unpleasant thought struck him.

"And there's no toilet in here. What happens when one of us needs a…"

"A horrifying prospect," said Ronnie, interrupting him. "So we may as well get started on the booze to take our minds off it. Your pledge to Diane to keep off it hardly matters anymore, does it? Why not have a beer? It'll make you feel better. Even if it is that cheap, vile stuff from those scabby working men's clubs you insist on frequenting."

Ronnie pulled a bottle of Wood Pit bitter from the crate and offered it to him. Bernard looked at it with fond memories. He recalled the taste of deliciously, hoppy loveliness, the flavours washing over his tongue and the joy of feeling it sliding down his throat. Maybe Ronnie was right? What harm could it do? They were stuck here, and there seemed little prospect of even seeing Diane ever again, let alone getting her back. The game was up, and he might as well accept it.

He looked at Ronnie, who was smiling as he held out the bottle. Should he take it? After all, he could just stop at one, couldn't he? Just one.

He took the bottle from Ronnie's hand.

Chapter Ten
June 1972

The Stranger could have stayed as long as he desired to torment Bernard and Ronnie. He was in the room of eternity after all. But he was impatient to return to the important tasks he had to perform if the plan for the resurrection of Fendara was to succeed. The first was to check on the progress of Jamset. His task had been to ensure all five descendants were brought to the house in their respective eras.

Jamset, just like the Stranger, was possessed of supernatural powers. Both possessed the ability to travel through time and to halt the ageing process. Ronnie and Bernard had been wrong when they had assumed the various versions of Jamset they had encountered had been ancestors or descendants of the one they had first met. There was but one, and he had been travelling between the time zones, keeping track of their progress.

Jamset was subservient to the Stranger who was Fendara's leading follower. The two of them had been preparing for the events that were to take place in the chamber for aeons and this night was to be the culmination of their centuries of work. He was busy preparing the chamber when the Stranger returned to check on his progress.

As the Stranger entered, the rocky ceiling slid smoothly open to reveal banks of sophisticated technology. From these, multicoloured lights began to flash in regular patterns onto the stone slab below, giving it an appearance reminiscent of a small dance floor in a nightclub.

"Ah, Jamset, how go the preparations?"

"The appointed hour is almost upon us. All has been prepared exactly according to your instructions."

"You have done well, Jamset. We have waited for thousands of years for this moment. Are all the victims prepared?"

"All except for Mr Bradshaw. He and his foolish friend continue to roam between the time zones. I tried to get them to stay in the drawing room but they keep wandering off. I fear that they may have become aware of our plans."

"Don't worry about Mr Bradshaw. I am letting him stew for a while to break his spirit. What about the others?"

"That Jocasta girl and her friend have been poking around in the drawing room, finding fault with everything, but they do not have an inkling of the real reason they are here. Nor have any of the others. When the moment has arrived they shall all be summoned to their positions. Then, when the clock strikes midnight and the stars are in alignment, our Lord Fendara shall be reborn."

"Excellent! And then he shall have his revenge on the whole world!"

The two of them cackled evilly, revelling in the prospect of what was to come. Meanwhile, outside the house, two more ne'er-do-wells were hatching a plot of their own. Compared with wreaking havoc on the world, though, what they had in mind was somewhat more mundane.

"Hold that torch straight, Ken," said Charlie who was messing around with a pair of bolt cutters next to a panel at the side of the house.

"Are you sure this is safe, Charlie?" asked Ken.

"Of course. I did my National Service in the Royal Engineers. I know how to handle live power lines. Now all I need to do is cut this and the house will be plunged into darkness. Then we can rock up at the front door and say we've come to fix it."

Ken shone the torch onto a jumble of wires as Charlie confidently cut through a large black cable. Simultaneously, two things happened. Firstly, all the lights in the house went off, just as Charlie had predicted. Unfortunately, he was also hit by a huge jolt of electricity and thrown back into a nearby hedge.

"Charlie, are you alright?" asked Ken, fearing the worst.

Charlie emerged from the hedge with a soot-blackened face and his hair standing on end. Things hadn't gone exactly as he had planned, but he had achieved his objective nonetheless.

He didn't know it, but his actions had temporarily thwarted Jamset and the Stranger's plans. In the chamber the flashing disco lights had gone out, much to their consternation. The only illumination remaining was from the flaming torches on the wall.

"What is the matter, why has the power failed?" asked the Stranger.

"I'm not sure. This is most irregular. I will go upstairs and investigate."

"See that you do, Jamset. Nothing must be allowed to stop this moment. Nothing!"

Jamset left the chamber through the 1972 arch. Back in the tower, Bernard was still staring temptation in the face as he contemplated the bottle of beer Ronnie had handed him.

"Come on, old skip, get it down you," urged Ronnie.

"I don't think I can," replied Bernard.

"Of course you can. You're not answerable to Diane anymore."

"That's not what I mean. The Stranger may be all-powerful but this is a metal cap and he didn't leave us a bottle opener. Perhaps it's a sign, to help me resist the temptation."

"Bloody inconsiderate, these apparitions, aren't they? Never mind, Rathbone rule number thirty-five, where there's a drink, there's a way."

"Hang on a minute. I thought you said rule thirty-five was never to go anywhere without a corkscrew. You know, I'm starting to suspect you're making these rules up as you go along."

"I assure you; I most certainly am not. You just aren't paying attention. Speaking of the corkscrew, I'm still annoyed that there wasn't one in the cellar when we first arrived. That Jamset was going out of his way to make it difficult for me to get a drink, giving me all that guff about the cook running out of sherry. I wouldn't have put it past him to have hidden it deliberately. If I see him again, I'm going to have it out with him."

"If we ever get out of here," said Bernard. "Here, you may as well have this back since I can't open it. And I don't want it anyway."

"Where there's a drink, there's a way, remember?"

Ronnie took the bottle back from Bernard and looked around the room, before alighting his eyes on the cell door which sported a huge lock with a large iron keyhole. He took the bottle over, wedged it into the hole and twisted.

There was a satisfying rush of carbon dioxide as the bottle opened, accompanied by the tinkle of the cap as it hit the floor. Triumphant, Ronnie turned back to Bernard.

"Got the bugger! Still, I'll have to amend my rule for future use. Never go anywhere without a corkscrew AND a bottle opener. Anyway, Bradders, here you go."

He handed the bottle back to Bernard which he eyed tentatively. At the same time, Ronnie picked up one of the bottles of rum, unscrewed the cap and held it up in his right hand.

"Right then, old chap. To the regiment!"

Ronnie held out his bottle to clink against Bernard's, who reluctantly complied. He was about to raise the beer to his lips when he noticed something behind Ronnie.

"Look! Behind you!"

"Oh come now, Bernard, what is this? A pantomime? Which, incidentally, is the lowest form of acting in my considered opinion."

"No! Look! The door's opening!"

"Are you sure?" asked Ronnie, turning around to see that the door was slowly swinging open, accompanied by a loud creaking sound that wouldn't have been out of place in a low-budget horror film. "How?"

"You must have somehow picked the lock when you stuck this beer bottle in it!" exclaimed Bernard.

"Yes, I guess I must," said Ronnie, warming to the idea that he may just have saved the day. "I'm rather a dab hand at this sort of thing, you know. Did you see that film I was in with Dickie Attenborough? The one where we escaped from Shietzen Castle? It was I who came up with the plan we used to trick the guard to get out of the cell."

"You were a non-speaking extra in that film," said Bernard, who had gone over to examine the door. "And I hate to shatter your illusions, but there's no lock on here at all. This keyhole is just for show. Not only that but he's also left it completely unguarded."

"Then what are we waiting for? Let's get out of here."

"Dead right," said Bernard, placing the bottle of beer on the ground. He had been so close to giving in to the temptation but now there was renewed hope, all desire for it had gone.

"You're not wasting that, are you?"

"You're welcome to it."

"Beer? Me? A Rathbone? I think not. But I still do not like to see good alcohol going to waste, even if it is of the working-class variety."

"I'm not touching it. The Stranger has been taunting me and trying to tempt me into taking a drink. Well, he hasn't succeeded. I didn't touch a drop. My pledge to Diane is still intact."

"An admirable sentiment, my boy, even if it is a pointless one. But I suppose a grudging amount of respect is due. You should be honoured. We Rathbones are hard taskmasters."

"I have never seen you give one iota of respect to anyone."

"It is the best way, old boy. Give them an inch and they'll take a mile. But get us out of this in one piece, preferably with a few quid in our pockets, and you'll have all the respect I can muster. Now come on, let's get moving. Remember what Bateson said. This is your chance to be a hero."

"Right you are."

"It's quite a way back to the house. I'd better hold on to this for the road," said Ronnie, clutching the bottle of rum as they exited the cell and climbed back up the steps to ground level.

"I would expect nothing less."

Reaching the front door first, Ronnie was pleased to see that the way out was clear.

"Our luck's in. This is unguarded too," said Ronnie. "There were a couple of big chaps out here when the Stranger brought me in."

"Oh, I dealt with them. They are probably still busy reciting their Lord's Prayers," replied Bernard.

"Eh?"

"Never mind, I'll explain later. Looking on the bright side, it's daylight out here again. So that will make getting back through the woods a tad easier."

"That just leaves that murderous chap with the musket to worry about, then," said Ronnie.

"Ah, well I have a theory about that," said Bernard. "I don't think he'll remember us if time has slipped back a couple of hours. All we need to do is sneak back undetected and go straight back down to the cellar."

They made their way back through the woods. Back in the chamber, the Stranger was standing at the dais in the centre of the chamber when the multicoloured lights above the slab came back on. A moment or two later, Jamset returned.

"Ah, Jamset. You have fixed the problem?"

"Yes, it should be fine now. It looks like someone has cut through the power lines outside. I have switched to the backup generator. I had it installed after all the power cuts last winter."

"Who could have cut the cables? It cannot have been Rathbone and Bradshaw because they are still in 1645."

"I am not sure. Bateson, perhaps? He has been a thorn in our side on many occasions."

"Not anymore. I've killed him. It matters not anyway as it is getting close to midnight. Nothing can stop us now. Are all the participants in the ceremony ready?"

"Each has taken possession of their version of the amulet in their respective time zones," replied Jamset. "We only need you to release Mr Bradshaw from his captivity and we shall have them all."

"Excellent! I have marooned him in time and imprisoned him with only his prattling friend and a crate of ale for company. If that doesn't break him, nothing will."

"If he is imprisoned, how will he get back here?"

"That's the beauty of it. They aren't even technically prisoners. They could walk out of that cell at any time. But whether it takes them an hour or a century to figure it out, it matters not. As soon as he leaves the tower, time will reset, giving him ample time to arrive back here. Once all five are in place, the circle will be complete."

"You have thought of everything, my lord."

"Of course I have, Jamset. That is why I am Fendara's leading disciple, and you are subservient to me. Now come, we cannot allow them to see us here until they are all assembled. We shall wait upstairs."

They left through one of the arches, just before Ronnie and Bernard emerged from another.

"Have you still got your trusty chalk, old chap?" asked Ronnie.

"Right here," replied Bernard, producing it from his pocket.

"Good, then mark that one, 1645."

Bernard chalked the date up above the arch, as they had with the others.

"That's it then, we've done them all," said Ronnie. "2022, 312, 1349 and 1645. So by process of elimination, this one must be 1972!"

He chalked the final couple of dates up above the arches.

"I hope so," said Bernard. "Much as I love history, I've seen quite enough of it for one evening."

"Agreed. So, let's go back upstairs and claim your inheritance."

"I don't think it's going to be that easy, Ronnie. Have you forgotten the ghosts, the time slips, the Romans, the Stranger, Bateson, Roundheads, murderous peasants, the Black Death, and the curse of Fendara who's about to destroy the world? I think we should forget about the inheritance, get the hell out of here, and be grateful we're still in one piece."

"Those were mere bumps in the road, my lad. We're on the home straight now. Come on, let's head for the drawing room and claim the loot."

He strode through the arch he had just marked 1972 leaving Bernard in his wake, as so often was the case.

They walked up the tunnel and into the cellar, which Ronnie was pleased to see was now once again fully stocked.

"You see, we're back where we belong, Bernard. Your vintage wine collection has returned! Surely you aren't going to turn your back on all this. I can drink it, even if you can't. Or we can sell it. Stuff like this goes for thousands."

Bernard lacked the energy to comment. The exertions of the last few hours had worn him out. He didn't know how Ronnie managed to keep going, seemingly sustaining himself completely on alcohol.

He would have to draw on reserves of strength from elsewhere. He hadn't succumbed to the temptation of the beer, despite all that had happened, so he wasn't beaten yet. Perhaps Bateson was right. He could be a hero and prevent the resurrection of Fendara. If he refused to claim the inheritance, and simply left, then surely he would be free of this crazy, haunted house and its curse.

And for the first time, he was beginning to think that he didn't need Diane either. Ronnie wasn't right about many things, but he had been right about her. It was time to let her go.

When they emerged from the cellar, they were relieved to see that the house was exactly as they had first seen it. They had indeed returned to 1972.

"Let's go now, Ronnie, while we still can."

"Now, let's not make any hasty decisions."

"I mean it. I want free of this place. I wish we had never come here."

Ronnie weighed up his options. Delaying tactics seemed like the best option.

"Very well if you insist. However, I need to go back to the drawing-room first. I think I left my pince-nez in there earlier when I was examining some of the ornaments."

This was a blatant lie. His pince-nez was safe in his pocket but it would buy him a little time. If Bernard was adamant about leaving, he could always steal a few more things from the house. It was full of priceless objects.

When they arrived back in the drawing room, Jamset was waiting for them.

"Where have you been, gentlemen? You were told to wait here."

"Less of your impertinence, Jamset," replied Ronnie. "We went in quest of sustenance. I can't wait around all evening on the off chance you might get around to bringing me a brandy at some point."

"Yes, and I feel it's only fair to tell you, I've decided not to stick around till midnight," added Bernard. "I've decided I don't want the inheritance now. I didn't mention this before but I had a call from Hollywood last week so I don't need the responsibility of this place. A big studio there has offered me a movie deal. I wasn't going to go because of Diane, but…"

"You don't know what you are saying, man," said Ronnie. "Pay no attention, Jamset, he's just spooked by some of the strange goings on this evening. I can assure you, he does want this inheritance."

"No, I don't," said Bernard. "So, if you don't mind, we'll be on our way."

"I'm afraid it is too late to change your mind now," replied Jamset. "As you can see, the waiting is almost over. Midnight shall soon be upon us."

He gestured at the grandfather clock which was showing that it was just before a quarter to the hour.

"I have to be here at midnight, not a quarter to," said Bernard. "We can be off the premises in plenty of time."

"If you say so, sir. But I think you will find that you will be here at midnight. You will have no choice."

"That sounds like a threat to me," said Bernard, eyeing Jamset carefully. There had been more than a hint of malice in his voice. "Are you going to force us to stay?"

"I shall not need to do that, sir. You will want to stay."

"I think you'll find I won't," said Bernard, who was now more determined than ever to leave.

And then, all of that changed. The clock gave out a single chime to signal that it was a quarter to midnight. As it did, Bernard's demeanour changed, His body stiffened, and he stood almost as if to attention and developed a strange, faraway look in his eyes. At the same time, the red amulet that had been in his pocket since he had first found it in the chamber, began pulsing.

This sudden alteration in behaviour didn't go unnoticed by Ronnie, even though he had been surreptitiously filling his pockets during the exchange between Bernard and Jamset.

"Bernard, what are you doing? You're not losing the plot again, are you?"

Bernard began to speak very slowly and deliberately, leaving long gaps between each word.

"I…must…go…to…the…chamber."

Each word was delivered with Bernard standing motionless, staring, unblinking in front of him.

"Why? We've only just come from there. And there's no need, see? I've still got half that bottle of rum I brought with me. We can see it out to midnight right here. This is a lovely room. It reminds me of a rather fine New Year's Eve party I had at Peter Sellers' house a few years back. Shame there are no women here."

"I…must…go…to…the…chamber. Diane is there."

"No, she isn't. Did you see her down there earlier? I didn't. This is some sort of trick. What have you done to him, Jamset?"

"He must fulfil his destiny," replied Jamset. "It is what he was born to do."

"He was born to be a third-rate comedian in a daytime soap opera. Now, I don't know what your game is but I for one do not believe a word of this rubbish about the world ending."

"Believe what you will, Mr Rathbone, but it will not change anything. He must go to the chamber and he must go now."

"Listen to me, Bernard," said Ronnie. "I don't know what this fellow's up to, but just in case there is some truth to all this, you need to stay away from that chamber. That's where all the trouble started. Then all will be well, you'll get your loot and we can all go home. Besides, I can't have the world ending yet. I think I'm on a promise with Josie in makeup. She said I had nice hair."

"You do not have any hair," said Jamset. "She was probably being sarcastic."

"No she wasn't," insisted Ronnie. "Tell him, Bernard."

"He has no interest in your trivialities," said Jamset. "His desire to return to the chamber overrides all other considerations."

Bernard started speaking again, slowly and calmly. There was no doubt in his mind about what he needed to do. It all made sense now.

"It is true. Diane is in the chamber. All I need to do is go down there and we'll be reunited. Then we'll be together, forever."

"Come on, look at this logically," said Ronnie. "How could she possibly be here? She doesn't even know where we are. You haven't spoken to her for weeks. Think about it."

"No. You are lying. You have been trying to keep us apart all this time. I see through it all now. I am going to find her and you cannot stop me."

Bernard began walking slowly and zombie-like towards the door.

"You must let him go, Mr Rathbone. He must fulfil his destiny," said Jamset.

"Don't listen, Bernard, he's trying to trick you," said Ronnie. "He's part of all this. Think about it. What was he doing in Roman times? This is all an elaborate trap and he has been trying to lure you into it ever since we came here."

But Bernard was long beyond listening. He stretched his arms out in front of him and speeded up, practically running towards the drawing-room door.

"Diane! I'm coming, love! I can hear you! Wait for me!"

An exasperated Ronnie was left with little choice but to follow. Meanwhile, similar scenes were unfolding across all the other time zones.

In Roman times, Cordelia had returned to the other Vestal Virgins but was now similarly afflicted to Bernard. It had begun when the red jewel in her chastity belt had begun pulsating to summon her.

"I must leave you, my sisters. I must go to the chamber."

The other virgins did not attempt to stop her, as she walked slowly ahead of her, with the same vacant stare in her eyes that Ronnie had seen in Bernard.

In 1349, the time zone in which there was no house, the Stranger had guided Samuel Blackwood through the trapdoor in the forest floor. As soon as he was inside, he advanced time to a quarter to midnight, causing the jewel he had been given to activate.

"This way, Samuel. Your destiny awaits!"

"Yes," replied Samuel. "I must join the others in the chamber."

The Stranger watched with satisfaction as Samuel made his way below ground.

Elsewhere Samuel's descendant, Thomas Blackwood, was being manipulated by Jamset in the newly built, luxurious drawing room of 1645.

"It is true, my lord. Cromwell himself is in the chamber beneath the house. This is your chance! Go down there, destroy him and the crown shall be restored!"

"Yes, I can see him in my mind, Jamset! I must go to the chamber!"

Possessed just like the others, Thomas took the chalice from the mantelpiece, left the drawing room, and made his way down through the cellar.

The final member of the group was Jocasta, who had spent much of the evening listening to Abigail's many arguments against her inheriting the house. This mostly involved examining various ornaments and items of décor and explaining their problematic nature.

Jocasta was tempted by the thought of the inheritance, but Abigail had been very persuasive. She had just about come around to the idea of leaving, when Jamset had arrived, bringing a tray of coffee and biscuits. Right away, Abigail began questioning him about the origins of the contents.

"Is this coffee fair trade?" she asked.

"Yes, I purchased it myself this morning, from Waitrose."

"And what about this sugar? Is it organic?"

"I can show you the packet if you so desire?"

"And the milk? Is it plant-based?"

It was the last question she had time to ask, as at that point the clock chimed for a quarter to midnight. As it did, Jocasta stiffened up as her amulet began to glow, just like the others. Then she began to speak.

"Abigail, you are right about this house. I see it all now. It was built by a very evil man! He was the one who brought all these vile things here."

"You see, I told you. I knew you'd come around to my way of thinking eventually."

"And what's more, he's down in the cellar right now. We must go there immediately and confront him."

"Sounds like a plan," said Abigail. It did not occur to her to question either how the builder of a house that was over three hundred years old could be present, or how Jocasta could know that he was. To her, it was another opportunity to lecture somebody, and those were not to be missed.

Jamset looked on in satisfaction as Jocasta, unblinking like the others, walked out of the room, and Abigail, seemingly oblivious to her friend's mental status, followed.

Soon, in all five time zones, the children of Fendara were below ground, making their way towards their final destination.

Chapter Eleven
June 1972

Back in 1972, Charlie and Ken were peering through the drawing room window which was once again lit up, thanks to Jamset restoring the power. Charlie was still looking somewhat the worse for wear after his recent shocking experience, and Ken wasn't convinced he had made a full recovery.

"Are you sure you're alright now, Charlie? I was worried you'd done a Valerie Barlow for a moment there."

"Yeah, I'm fine. But I've had enough of this nonsense. I'm just about ready to give that Ronnie a pasting. Shame they got the power back on, but never mind. Let's just go in anyway. There doesn't seem to be anyone about."

"I thought he had until next Friday to pay up," replied Ken.

"You know as well as I do, Ken, they never pay up. We're here now, we might as well do the job. Plus, it looks like there are a few tasty antiques in there. We won't go back to the Colonel empty-handed."

Ken nodded eagerly. He liked a job that involved hurting pcoplc but most of them were the dregs of society who nobody gave two figs about. But the chance to do over a television star? It would be the crowning moment of his career. Hungry for the violence to come, he began to follow Charlie, who was already making his way around to the front door.

The front door was unlocked, so they let themselves into the deserted hallway.

"Now, where is he hiding?" asked Charlie, as they began to make their way across the hall.

Downstairs in the chamber, a single, funereal bell was tolling. The multi-coloured lights were dancing on the slab, whilst steam billowed all around. Then, all five of Fendara's descendants emerged from the arches simultaneously and proceeded, still completely zombie-like, towards the centre.

All were either wearing or carrying their amulets which began to glow ever brighter. They continued to walk slowly towards the slab, as Ronnie and Abigail also emerged from their respective time zones. Their eyes met and both instinctively threw the other a look of disgust.

So she did remember him after all. So much for the theory about the time reset wiping her memory. But Ronnie knew this was no time to indulge in another round of verbal sparring with her. The situation was deadly serious.

"Bernard, speak to me. What's happening?"

Bernard did not turn around, but he did reply.

"Do not interfere, Ronnie. My whole life has been leading up to this moment. In a few minutes, we shall be reunited."

"We? Who are we?"

"All five of us. We shall be as one."

Ronnie might have been aware of the gravity of the situation, but Abigail wasn't. She hadn't been through the trials and tribulations that he had and hadn't quite grasped what was going on.

"Jocasta, where's the evil man you told me about? Is it this misogynistic monstrosity we met earlier? I knew there was something wrong about him."

"Do you mean me?" asked Ronnie, looking behind him to check there wasn't anyone else there.

"I most certainly do and let me tell you, I've got a weekly column in *The Guardian* and by the time I've finished with you, the whole world will know what a monster you are!"

"Silence, foolish child," said Jocasta, to Abigail's surprise. "You have no idea what is happening here, have you? How appalling to see all that intellectual capacity going to waste. Still, all of you will be going to waste soon, as well as the rest of your pathetic kind. Come, brethren, let us join hands."

The five of them linked hands and closed in tighter around the centre of the room as the steam grew more intense around them, billowing up almost above their heads. As it did, there was a deafening sound resembling a church bell beginning to strike the twelve peals of midnight. It was so loud, Ronnie felt almost as if he was within the bell tower itself and he flung his hands over his ears to block out the sound.

Abigail was similarly afflicted, though the five linking hands around the slab seemed unaffected. They both looked around for the source, but there was no bell or clock present in the room as far as either could see.

Then a whirlwind began to form above the central slab, growing rapidly in intensity. The link between the five descendants was broken and they fell backwards as the shape of a body began to form, standing upright within the whirlwind. Ronnie watched, fascinated, as its face began to form. It took only a few seconds for him to recognise it.

"Jamset?" he inquired.

"No," replied the coalescing apparition. "I am Fendara. Jamset was merely a projection of myself, seeded through time to help bring you all here. Now, at last, I shall be reborn! And the whole of the human race that imprisoned me here shall suffer for all eternity at my hands."

"And what of the one they call the Stranger? The one who kidnapped me?"

"He is here. Look!"

Fendara pointed to the rear of the cellar where the Stranger was gaping open-mouthed at the apparition in front of him. All these years he had thought that Jamset had been serving him. Now he realised it had been the other way around all along.

"My Lord Fendara!" he exclaimed. "You have returned, just as the prophecy foretold. I am at your service."

"Thank you," said Fendara. "But I don't need you anymore. You can go, quite literally to hell."

Fendara pointed a finger at the Stranger, who with a sinking feeling realised what was to come.

"No, my lord! I have served you faithfully throughout the centuries. Destroy these others, by all means, but spare me!"

"I don't think so," said Fendara, as a fireball shot out and his faithful servant was blown into a pile of bones.

"That was a bit harsh," observed Ronnie, who couldn't resist a joke, despite the prospect of imminent death. "An eternity of service and that's what you get. Couldn't you have just given him a carriage clock or something?"

"Your prattling will be the end of you," said Fendara. "Very, very soon. As for the Stranger, I didn't kill him anyway. He was nothing but a bag of bones I took from a grave, reassembled into the form of the Reaper, and resurrected. Now I have no further use for him, he has returned whence he came."

"So your conscious is clear?"

"I do not possess one. But even if I did, I would have no qualms about killing you, little man."

"Little? I'm a good six foot, I'll have you know."

"I was referring to your persona rather than your physical dimensions. You shall be the next to die and it will be an absolute pleasure. I've been aching to do it ever since you insulted me with your mock Indian accent when you first arrived. I'll be doing the world a favour getting rid of you. Well, temporarily at least. Until I kill all of them as well."

He raised his hand again and unleashed another bolt of lightning, but Ronnie somehow managed to duck out of the way. It was amazing how quickly he could move when saving his skin depended on it.

"Not bloody, likely. Come on, Bernie old cocker, time to go."

He snapped his fingers in front of Bernard's eyes, but his friend did not move.

"No, Ronnie. I must stay. All of us must stay."

"Suit yourself, but I'm off," he replied before turning to Abigail and adding, "and so should you if you've got any sense."

"I would rather perish here than go anywhere with you," she replied.

"Die, little man!" said Fendara, preparing to unleash another bolt. But he was still not fully formed in the whirlwind and his coordination was poor. He struggled to focus his aim on Ronnie as he ran around the chamber, dodging the next firebolt as he went. He turned to run towards the arch marked 1972, but was stopped in his tracks by the sudden appearance of Ken and Charlie in the archway.

"There he is!" yelled Charlie.

"Get him!" called Ken.

Ronnie changed course, and headed back across the room, deciding to make for the 2022 archway instead, figuring that was the safest option. Ken followed him, whilst Charlie rushed across the other side, hoping to cut him off. He was determined to get his hands on Ronnie first, but in his enthusiasm, he tripped and fell directly onto the slab, right into the glowing whirlwind which contained the still-forming image of Fendara.

Instantly, things changed. The whirlwind turned a bright red colour, Charlie vanished completely, and the image of Fendara began to fizz and crackle, like a television losing reception. His face also became unstable, morphing rapidly between Jamset, Bernard, Cordelia, Samuel, Thomas, and Jocasta. Then briefly, it took on the form of Charlie.

"No!" screamed Fendara. "My DNA! It must be pure."

As the creature struggled within the whirlwind, it fired off a random bolt of lightning which incinerated Ken, leaving just a smoking pile of ashes where he had been standing just a moment before, wondering what had happened to his partner.

While Fendara was struggling to re-establish his true form, the spell on his five descendants was temporarily broken. Bernard, coming to his senses, looked around him, bewildered as to what was going on.

"Where's Diane?" he asked. For some reason, he was under the impression that she was in the chamber, but looking around he couldn't see her. Just a collection of people, most of whom he had met in the various time zones.

Fendara continued to crackle and fizz, with the impurity caused by Charlie's unexpected intervention, but had now stabilised his appearance, once again into that of Jamset.

"Poor deluded fool! That was just an illusion to get you down here. Diane is gone, gone from your life, as your ridiculous friend has tried to tell you countless times. You have only ever had one purpose, to be part of my rebirth, and now you have fulfilled that function. Remember three weeks ago when you took the overdose?"

"You took an overdose?" asked a surprised Ronnie. "You never told me about that, Bernard."

"I didn't tell anyone. Why would I? It's not the sort of thing you broadcast."

"But I knew," said Fendara. "I know all and I see all. I have been watching you for years. I know all your habits and your movements and I have been tormenting you.

Now you are in pain and you no longer want to live, so now I bring you Fendara's gift of death!"

"But I don't want to die," said Bernard. "That's why I forced myself to throw up those tablets."

"At my direction," said Fendara. "I could not have you dying before you had served your purpose."

Despite his threats, Fendara was still struggling to take corporeal form. By now he should be fully materialised and crushing these puny humans. But Charlie's intervention had well and truly thrown a spanner into the works. Not only was he struggling to keep control, but to make matters worse, he sensed another supernatural presence entering the chamber which he lacked the power to suppress. He watched, incensed as the ghostly image of Bateson appeared in front of the arch that led to 1349.

"He is correct, young sir," said Bateson. "As I told you when you visited me in my cave, you are part of the crooked line. That is why you are here. But Fendara got one crucial detail wrong. You are not here to resurrect him, but to put an end to this evil, once and for all!"

"Silence, old man!" screamed Fendara. "How can you be here? My servant the Stranger destroyed you!"

He let off a firebolt straight at Bateson but it went right through him. The image was merely a projection.

"Bernard, this is your moment!" said Bateson. "Be the hero you always wanted to be."

"Umm, I'm not sure I know how," said Bernard.

"You are more powerful than you think, seize this moment. The past is gone, let it go, and start again. The future is a wonderful place and it's waiting for you."

The whirlwind containing Fendara finally began to stabilise. The crackling stopped and finally began to solidify. Bernard knew he didn't have much time. Summoning reserves of strength he never knew he had, he turned to face his enemy, spurred on by the old seer's words.

"Bateson was right! You are evil and you've been interfering in my life all this time. Now it's time to banish you once and for all."

"Do you think you can stop me, puny human? I'm not the cause of your unhappiness. You wrecked your own life. Look at you, 'Barrel of Laughs' Bradshaw, everybody's best mate, cracking the jokes. But they're all laughing at you, not with you."

The weaker, depressed Bernard he used to be would have been cut to pieces by these words, but with his renewed sense of vigour, they simply washed over him. He knew his enemy was merely taunting him and trying to break him, just as he had when he had locked him up in the tower. Well, it wasn't going to work.

"You lie, Fendara! You're trying to make me doubt myself, but it won't work on me anymore. I'm going to put a stop to your evil, once and for all."

"I think it is more likely I shall put a stop to you. This is your curtain call. Don't be sad. It's what you wanted, remember? Diane doesn't want you, so why go on? It's time to take your final bow."

Maybe what Bernard was about to do would be his final bow, but he reasoned that at least he would die like a man. He had no idea what effect his next action was going to have, though there was a strong chance it was going to mean the end of his life. But nothing was going to stop him now.

"Perhaps it will be, Fendara! But if I go down, I'm taking you with me."

He launched himself onto the slab and grappled with the semi-formed body of Fendara. It was curiously malleable to the touch, as if he was wrestling with a man wearing a wetsuit full of jelly, but he was determined not to let go. He shoved Fendara out of the whirlwind and off the slab, a move which produced a loud cry from his enemy.

Away from the protection of the whirlwind, and with the contamination of Charlie's DNA corrupting the partially formed body, Fendara was unable to stabilise himself. He screamed one last scream as his features and then his entire body began to dissolve, melting away into the floor of the chamber. It was as if someone had thrown an ice sculpture into a pool of boiling water. Within half a minute, all trace of him was gone.

"Bravo, old boy! I knew you had it in you!" said Ronnie, applauding as the others in the chamber looked on.

Bernard was temporarily dazed after his epic encounter and fell backwards, but Ronnie caught him.

"Bernard? Are you OK? Speak to me, boy!"

Once again he did his trick of snapping his fingers in front of Bernard's eyes, and this time it worked as his friend opened his eyes and spoke.

"You know, if I didn't know you better, I'd almost have believed that was some genuine concern you were showing there."

Although Fendara was gone, the dancing lights were still present and becoming brighter. The smoke was also increasing and there was a loud rumbling sound all around them. Then there was the sound of a large crack and a thick cloud of dust fell from the ceiling, directly onto Ronnie's head.

"What's happening?" asked Cordelia, who like the others had been shaken out of her reverie.

"Bernard here is a hero!" proclaimed Ronnie proudly. "He's just saved all our lives. But I fear we may not be out of the woods just yet. I get the feeling that we may need to get out of here rather sharpish. And you know what that means, my boy, don't you?"

"Not more running, please? I've just grappled with the evillest creature in the history of the world. Can't you give me a minute to get my breath back?"

"This will be the last time, old chap, I promise."

Ronnie turned to address the others.

"Now listen to me, all of you, you need to run for your lives! Go out through the arch marked with your year on it and get as far away from here as possible. Hurry!"

For once, Abigail didn't argue with him. She was as keen to get out of there as anyone, and ran through the 2022 arch, with Jocasta in hot pursuit. Samuel and Thomas also departed without another word, but Cordelia turned back to say her farewells.

"Goodbye, Ronnie!"

"Goodbye, my dear. Such a shame we couldn't get better acquainted. Oh, your arch is 312 by the way."

Cordelia, much to his surprise, ran up to him and gave him a quick peck on the cheek before running through her arch. Bernard looked at him in amazement, but if anything Ronnie was even more surprised. It seemed as if she genuinely liked him and it had been a while since he had been able to say that about a woman. And it wasn't just because she was in it for the money, he was sure of that. But there was no time to linger. They had to get out of there.

They ran through the tunnel and back into the cellar, by which time things were getting decidedly precarious. There were chunks of masonry falling all around and they only just managed to get up the steps that led to the hallway before the entire staircase cracked and collapsed behind them.

Back on the ground floor, the rumbling was growing ever stronger. Bernard was in front and headed straight for the front door where he was delighted to see the Jepson, right where they had left it. He looked back, but Ronnie wasn't behind him. What had happened to him now? Had he fallen over again?

He didn't fancy going back in to look for him but it looked as if he was going to have no choice. The whole house was wobbling and looked as though it could collapse at any moment. It seemed he was going to have to play the hero one last time.

Then, just as he was steeling himself to go back in, Ronnie emerged from the front door, pockets bulging and carrying a large picture frame. There was no time to ask questions. Bernard leapt in and started the car and waited with the engine running. Ronnie opened the rear door, threw in the painting and a few other trinkets, and clambered in behind him.

"Drive!" he urged.

Bernard needed no encouragement, slamming the car into gear and accelerating up the gravel driveway, wheels spinning and screeching as they went.

When they reached the top of the drive, Bernard looked into the mirror to behold an incredible sight. The house was no longer merely wobbling, it was warping into a narrower shape as if it were being forced into a funnel.

"Look, Ronnie," he said, stopping the car at what he hoped was a safe distance.

They watched as the entire house was sucked into a vortex into the ground, before vanishing completely. Where it had stood there was nothing left, just a bare, grassy field.

"Well, that's that, then," said Ronnie, lighting up a cigarette. "Shame about you losing your house and the inheritance, but it could have been worse."

"I'm not bothered about the money, Ronnie. The important thing is, we stopped Fendara."

"You stopped him, old chap. It pains me to say this, because you know I always play the hero in my dramatic roles, but I'm gracious enough to concede that you had the starring role today. I always knew you could do it."

"I'm not even sure exactly what it was I did yet," replied Bernard. "One thing, I can't figure out is why did those two men turn up? You know, the ones who we met in the studio bar? They were heavies, weren't they?"

"Possibly," said Ronnie, reluctant to admit the truth.

"Be honest, Ronnie, you're in financial trouble. That's why you were so keen on me getting the inheritance. You wanted me to bail you out."

"Well, that's not a problem anymore, old thing. I managed to liberate a few items on the way out. Cop a load of this lot."

Ronnie reached into his pocket to reveal various valuables he had pilfered from the house, including a solid gold pocket watch.

"Oh and there's this of course," he said, picking up the painting. "I noticed it on the way out. It's an old master, you know. Worth thousands. Though technically, these things are yours, of course."

"Keep them and sell them. I don't need the money. And I don't need Diane anymore either. She's made her choice. I see now she wasn't the angel I convinced myself she was. Messing around with that sound engineer, for example. I was blind to it. Blinded by love. It's all going to be different from now on, I can tell you."

"Aah! Bernie! Bernie, old boy, you've come back to me. I knew you would. But what about your new film career in Hollywood? You're not really leaving me, are you?"

"Of course not. I just made that up. I was trying to come up with a valid excuse to give Jamset to justify leaving before midnight."

"What? Are you telling me you lied and boasted to make your career sound more important than it is?"

"Well, you should know! You do it all the time."

"I confess, I may elaborate on occasion. Never mind, all is well that ends well. You're staying, we have all this loot from the house and there's one other thing too. You remember that man the heavies were with the other night?"

"The one you said was an agent?"

"Yes. I told a little white lie there. He's known as the Colonel, and he's the one I'm in hock to. But thanks to Brian's phone, I've got a little surprise for him. It's all coming up roses, dear boy, all coming up roses."

And with that, they drove away into the night.

Chapter Twelve
June 1972

Five days later Ronnie and Bernard were back on set, filming the final scenes of the latest episode of *Sladen Street*.

"I'm sorry, Mr Crispin, but that's my final offer!" said Bernard firmly.

"You drive a hard bargain, Tommy. I shall have to sleep on it," replied Ronnie intensely.

"See that you do!" exclaimed Bernard dramatically. "Or it could be the end of Crispin's – forever!"

They stared at each other, trying not to blink or move for the final freeze frame, with sombre looks on their faces.

"And, cut!" called the director. "OK, everybody, that's a wrap!"

Bernard and Ronnie relaxed and walked off the set.

"Coming to the bar, old fruit?" asked Ronnie.

"Possibly, but I just need to have a word with Verity first about my trousers," said Bernard. "They're getting far too loose."

"Well, let's hope they don't fall down while you're talking to her like mine did that time."

"Yes, but that was deliberate, Ronnie. I think I must be losing weight. It's amazing what staying off the booze can do for you. Then there was all that running at the weekend."

"Off you go, then. Still off the sauce?"

"For now. And you should cut down too."

"Perhaps, old chap, but not tonight. I'm in a celebratory mood. I'll get you a Coke or something. But not a diet one, eh?"

"Hardly. They haven't invented it yet."

"The future was a fascinating place, wasn't it? What do you think happened to all the people we met?"

"They went back to their own time, I guess. It's all very peculiar, though. I made some enquiries and there is no evidence that the house ever existed."

"Apart from the stuff we took from it. Thankfully that didn't disappear," said Ronnie, much to his relief.

"Indeed," replied Bernard.

He wandered off to talk to Verity, as Ronnie made his way off the stage towards the door that led to the bar. But before he reached it, he was confronted by the Colonel who was accompanied by two new heavies. They looked even larger and dumber than the previous two.

What was he doing in here? It was one thing security letting him into the bar, but how had he managed to get onto the set? The man seemed to be able to go wherever he liked. Not that Ronnie minded, on this occasion. He had been expecting to encounter him in the bar, but this would do just as well.

"Aah, Ronald, I must say, your performance was superlative this evening," began the Colonel.

"Thank you, one does one's best, given the paucity of the material. What brings you here?"

"It's Friday, Ronald, remember? Payday. I do hope we're not going to have a problem?"

"No, not at all."

He reached into his pocket and, to the Colonel's amazement, pulled out a thick roll of Scottish one hundred-pound notes.

"Here you go, five large, plus interest. No need to count it, it's all there."

"Well, Ronald. I'm flabbergasted. Lance, Percival, I'm afraid I shall not need your services tonight."

The two heavies grumbled under their breath.

"Don't worry, boys, you'll get paid regardless and there are plenty of other folks we need to see this weekend who I doubt will be so forthcoming. You'll see plenty of action tomorrow."

Lance and Percival seemed more cheerful at this suggestion.

"By the way, Ronald, you haven't seen Ken and Charlie anywhere, have you? They seem to have disappeared. I just wondered if you might have bumped into them last weekend at some point."

"Nope, not a sausage, I'm afraid. Listen, now I've paid up, my credit's all good again, isn't it?"

"Of course. You're one of my most valued customers. Whatever it is you want, you need only to ask."

"Good, because there's a horse I fancy running in the Northumberland Plate tomorrow. It's called Scoria. I was hoping to have a substantial investment. A thousand, shall we say? On the nose?"

"It will be my pleasure!" exclaimed the Colonel, marvelling at Ronnie's stupidity. He would never learn. But who was he to argue? If he wanted to get himself back into debt again, he would be more than happy to accommodate him.

"Excellent, so just to confirm, that's one thousand pounds to win on Scoria at the starting price for the Northumberland Plate at Newcastle tomorrow."

"Confirmed," said the Colonel.

"Might I have a receipt? I know a gentleman's word is his bond and all that, but it helps keep it all above board, doesn't it?"

"Not a problem," said the Colonel, who pulled out a notebook and pen, jotted down the details of the bet and then handed it over to Ronnie."

"Good, well I believe that concludes our business," said Ronnie.

"Thank you, Ronald. Always a pleasure. Come along, Lance and Percival."

The Colonel and his employees departed, just as Bernard returned from his chat with Verity.

"That was that chap, wasn't it?" said Bernard. "The one you owe money to. Have you paid him off? Who is he, exactly?"

"A rather odious turf accountant. But thanks to your generosity, he's now off my case."

"I knew he wasn't an agent the second I clocked him. I trust you're all straight now and I hope you've learnt your lesson. If I can stay off the booze, then I don't see any reason you can't give the nags a rest."

"Calm yourself, dear boy. That painting fetched a tidy sum, more than enough to pay off the debt. Not only that, now I've got that crook right where I want him."

"How come?"

"It's all thanks to that fanboy Brian, and his fantastic little gadget. I looked up the winner of the big race at Newcastle this weekend on his phone, not to mention loads of other big races over the next few years. I forecast that our friend the Colonel is in for a run of bad luck,"

"Hmmm, as long as he doesn't break your legs."

"The Colonel may be a thug but he is a man of honour," replied Ronnie.

"Good. And by the way, there was one other thing I wanted to tell you. The day after we got back, can you believe it, I really did get a call from Hollywood!"

"So you're going after all, then?"

"Nope. I've decided to pass on it."

"Really? Are you sure?"

"Yes. I've thought about it a lot and I've decided to stay here with you. After all, you stood by me in my hour of need, and it would be wrong of me to run out on you now."

"Indeed it would," said Ronnie. He hadn't told him the truth about Terrance not giving him a new contract. Would Bernard have stayed if he had known?

"Yes, and now the strike's over, Terrance says he'll give me a twelve-month contract at twice the pay if I stay."

"Have you given him your answer yet?"

"No, I told him I'm mulling it over. But he's desperate to keep me."

"I'm sure he is," said Ronnie, spotting an opportunity to turn the situation to his advantage. "Listen, old chum, I think you should accept, but with one proviso. Tell him you'll only stay for another year if he keeps me on as well."

"Hasn't he offered you a new contract yet?"

"Oh, it's a mere formality, my boy. Not even up for discussion. He just hasn't got around to it yet. But if you insist, on it as a condition of your contract, how can he say no?"

"Right you are, then."

"Oh, and while you're at it, tell him I want my salary doubled too. It's only fair."

"Consider it done."

"And now, dear chap, I suggest we repair to the bar. I feel like splashing some of my newfound wealth about."

"Just a quick one, then. I promised to take that new girl out to a club later. I think she might be the one!"

He gestured across to a slim, dark-haired girl in a yellow miniskirt, taking notes on a clipboard from the director. She looked up, caught Bernard's eye, and smiled.

"Well don't go rushing in like a bull in a china shop," said Ronnie. "Remember what happened last time. On the other hand, if it helps get Diane out of your system, go for it."

"Diane who?" said Bernard, with a mischievous twinkle in his eye.

"That's my boy," replied Ronnie. "Enjoy."

"I will," said Bernard. "I'll just go and tell her we'll be ready to go in half an hour."

Ronnie watched with some amusement as Bernard made his way over to his potential new love interest.

Doubtless he would end up getting his heart broken again, but there was nothing he could do about it. If the lad wouldn't follow the Rathbone rules, he had only himself to blame.

Speaking of the Rathbone rules, he checked his watch. He would have to get a move on or he would be in breach of rule number ten: always be in the bar at least half an hour before last orders.

Feeling content with the way things had worked out, he made his way out of the studio and headed for the bar.

THE END – but Ronnie and Bernard will return in *The Haunted Theatre*.

Further Reading

If you've enjoyed *The Crooked Line*, you may be pleased to hear that I have another time travel series entitled The Time Bubble. This has been going strong since 2014 and now stretches to over a dozen books. Details can be found on the next page.

Also, if you could be kind enough to leave me a review or a rating on Amazon at some point, that would be hugely appreciated. As an independent author, I rely on word of mouth to spread the word about my books, plus genuine reviews from enthusiastic readers who have enjoyed them.

Thanks for reading!

Jason.

The Time Bubble Collection

To find out more about my other series, please head over to my author page on Amazon where you can find the books individually, or in box sets:

1) The Time Bubble
2) Global Cooling
3) Man Out of Time
4) Splinters in Time
5) Class of '92
6) Vanishing Point
7) Midlife Crisis
8) Rock Bottom
9) My Tomorrow, Your Yesterday
10) Happy New Year
11) Return to Tomorrow
12) Cause of Death
13) Lauren's Odyssey

UK Link:

https://www.amazon.co.uk/Jason-Ayres/e/B00CQO4XJC/

US Link:

https://www.amazon.com/Jason-Ayres/e/B00CQO4XJC/

About the Authors

Jason Ayres spends his days writing humorous novels with science fiction elements, including time travel and alternate realities. He has yet to win the Booker Prize but did achieve fame back in 2013 when the title of Britain's Official Sausage Taster was bestowed upon him.

You can sign up for his newsletter at his website:

https://www.jasonayres.co.uk

Or find him on social media:

https://twitter.com/TheTimeBubble/
https://www.facebook.com/TheTimeBubble/

Michael Livesley is an actor, singer, writer, and comedian once described by Stephen Fry as "an outrageous talent." He is also one half of the *Nice Things* show – the antidote to modern living on YouTube:

https://www.youtube.com/michaellivesley

Find him on Twitter here:

https://twitter.com/MichaelLivesley

Printed in Great Britain
by Amazon